Mary Anne brought her blanket. She brought to-morrow's clothes out of the pack and then went down to the spring to wash her face. She made a big production of preparing herself for John Slocum.

Mary Anne was very annoyed to see her gallant knight already dozing off under the stars.

"A gentleman never falls asleep on a lady," she complained.

"Maybe so. But we ain't them," Slocum replied.

He pulled his socks off and rolled his shirt over his broad shoulders. It gave her the shivers—the sight of the power in his back. At once, she was ready for love.

OTHER BOOKS BY JAKE LOGAN

JAKE LOGAN

SILVER CITY SHOOTOUT

BERKLEY BOOKS, NEW YORK

SILVER CITY SHOOTOUT

A Berkley Book / published by arrangement with
the author

PRINTING HISTORY
Berkley edition / April 1983

ISBN: 0-425-06132-9

A BERKLEY BOOK ® TM 757,375
Berkley Books are published by Berkley Publishing Corporation,
200 Madison Avenue, New York, N.Y. 10016.
The name ''Berkley'' and the stylized ''B'' with design are trademarks
belonging to Berkley Publishing Corporation.

PRINTED IN THE UNITED STATES OF AMERICA

1

Muleshoe's Bums—that's what they called them. And old Smitty, the cook, had to admit the truth of it. Their horses were magnificent, because the spread they were riding for didn't own any low-grade horse-flesh. But the riders were the scruffiest, sorriest bunch of hands west of the Rockies.

It was October, eighteen and seventy-one, high in the Owyhee Mountains: country that would later become part of the state of Idaho.

One of the riders was shivering. Smitty knew he'd shiver until he found the little bottle in his saddlebag and nipped at it. The rider, Fat Matthews, had a perfectly good buffalo coat rolled up behind his saddle, but even though winter comes early in the high country, he never remembered to put it on. Matthews went through half a dozen of those little bottles every day. Maybe he only got cold on the inside.

Smitty sat up high on the chuck-wagon seat and clucked at the two big jack mules who drew it. On his flank, a bunch of sheep scattered down an alder draw; the foreman, Jack Renfrew, was right after them, riding hell-for-leather.

Renfrew made no secret of his feeling for the huge flock of animals in his charge. Renfrew was a cowman; often he said so. He hated the sheep; often he said so. He wished Muleshoe would sell off the flock and buy into the cattle business.

Woolies killed the grass, and cattle wouldn't graze or water once woolies had passed. Every cowpuncher worth his saddle knew those home truths. Renfrew's quarter horse crashed through the rear ranks of the fleeing sheep, and if the hooves smashed one or two of the damn critters, then that was their hard luck. He came to the head of the band, turning into them. They all stopped dead and stared at him. Damn woolies, anyway! Now, a cow would already be retracing its steps up the draw, but these damn sheep didn't know enough to do as they ought. They just stared at the foreman, their eyes wide with fear. The foreman cursed. He beat his hat against his legs. Jack Renfrew rushed his horse at them and they scattered. Moving too fast to do very much good, he chased them down, yelled at them, waved and slapped his hat, and slowly the sheep returned to the main flock.

Sheep had come to this country in the late sixties, and there wasn't a cowman for five hundred miles didn't curse them. That was when Muleshoe was a perfectly respectable outfit. The kind of outfit any man could be proud to work for. Two thousand acres of hay bottom and god knows how many miles of unfenced range.

Cows hadn't been doing so well the last few years, and some of the bigger outfits—High and Stout, Davis Cattle Co., and Rolling D—had gone under. Muleshoe sold its cattle and bought sheep.

Renfrew trotted past the chuck wagon, his eyes on the white mass of animals for others likely to break.

Smitty called, "Don't push 'em so hard. They can't move so fast as cows do."

Well, Jack Renfrew wasn't one to take advice gracefully. "Old man, don't tell me how to handle livestock," he snapped.

"Suit yourself." Smitty popped his reins, which caused no alteration in the pace of the big jacks that pulled him and his wagonload of necessaries.

Smitty was the wrong side of sixty. During the war, already an old-timer, he'd ridden with Quantrill's guerrillas, and he loved to yarn about those times and the men who'd gone on to fame—or notoriety, depending on how you looked at it.

Most of the other punchers paid Smitty no mind. Smitty and Renfrew were the only permanent crew Muleshoe had sent on this gather. Renfrew had hired the rest of the bums in Soda Springs—paid off their whiskey debts and sobered them up and tied them to their horses when they weren't sober enough to stay aboard themselves.

Only the Kid appreciated Smitty's stories. Maybe he had a real name once—first, middle, and last—but that was back east, where he'd come from. Out here he was known simply as the Kid.

He wasn't but sixteen—and a scrawny, underfed sixteen at that. The old Colt Dragoon he wore strapped to his skinny leg looked to have more weight than any other part of him.

How he loved that Colt! After a hard day riding after the sheep, collecting them, re-collecting them, shoving them a few miles down the trail, the Kid would pull the charges on his Colt, clean it, oil it lightly, work over the hammer with a hone until the trigger was so light a damn feather could have set it off. All the while he'd listen to Smitty yarning about the great gunfighters: Frank and Jesse James, the Younger brothers, John Slocum, and Bill Anderson himself. "Oh, they was like the knights of old." That's how Smitty finished his stories. "Men to ride the river with."

The half-breeds hung together around the fire, impassive unless they were jabbering at each other in that Indian lingo of theirs. And then there were the two Spaniards, Ortiz and his son; they hung together too. The halfwit Billy, Fat Matthews, Whiskey Bill, Smitty, and the Kid—Muleshoe's Bums.

The foreman, Jack, always ate by himself and never offered a word that wasn't business. He meant to get these sheep down the trail onto the Camas Prairie and return to the ranch headquarters where he could break horses or ride line fence or do any of the work that a real cowboy should. When Muleshoe bought sheep, everybody quit except for Renfrew and Smitty, the belly robber. Renfrew would have quit except for Mary Anne Murchison, who was too fine a woman and too sensitive to be abandoned. Mr. Murchison himself, old J.D., had a bum ticker. He'd passed out twice on the street and never ever rode horseback anymore. He traveled in the surrey or buckboard with somebody else to do the driving.

So Renfrew planned to stick around. He was just twenty-five, which was young for foreman of a spread as big as Muleshoe. Eight thousand sheep. Biggest flock in the territory. Old J.D. called them the wave of the future, and had every bit of their wool contracted to mills out on the coast who wove greatcoats and blankets for the U.S. Army. It was the wool that made them valuable. Renfrew never knew anybody to eat a sheep. Personally, he'd sooner eat a magpie, feathers and all.

Nights were cool. The aspen leaves were brilliant red, and the cottonwoods had dropped theirs. A couple times, crossing some deer meadow, a few woolies would go crazy—running around butting each other before they frothed at the mouth and died. After he figured it out, Renfrew didn't let them linger or graze in the meadows where the lupine hung their golden seed pods. With graze scarce this late in the season, those pods looked pretty good to the sheep—but they were poison, sure enough.

The days were still warm. From time to time a wind'd come up and get under your collar and chill you to let you know winter was on the way.

Craggy mountains at their back. Crystalline mountain streams (before the sheep crossed them) and deer meadows. Plenty game. Just yesterday the Kid had brought down an elk. They took the loin and one leg and left the rest for the wolves. Maybe if they were fed up a little they wouldn't bother the sheep.

Except for calving time or when the weather was god-awful, wolves didn't bother cattle much. Catamounts and bears would kill a cow, but wolves generally left them alone. But sheep were just their meat, and every night the nighthawks riding around the enormous flock watched the eyes. Golden eyes waiting for their chance to leap in and take a ewe.

One good thing you could say about the sheep—they didn't stampede. A nighthawk could shoot him a couple of wolves, and the nearest sheep would get to their feet and move away a short distance and lie down again. Cattle would have stampeded in a minute.

Since Muleshoe wasn't buying any man's ammunition, the only one doing any wolf killing was the Kid. One morning, at the chuck wagon, he said, "I suppose you'll be calling me the Wolf Kid from now on." He laughed, but everybody knew he wanted to be called the Wolf Kid and didn't think it was a joke.

Two nights ago Smitty had been nighthawking the far side of the flock (he kept wanting to call it a "herd") from the Kid. He was sleepy after working all day and half dozed while his horse made the rounds around the placid woolies. He woke up sudden when he heard the Kid's voice: "Come out of there you sonofabitch or I'll shoot your lights out."

The Kid was dismounted. His horse, ground reined, waited behind him. The Kid was in the gunfighter's crouch and naught to see but the pine trees, the mountains, and the wolf eyes.

Smitty grinned.

The Kid drew, pretty quick, and his pistol spoke once, twice. Out of the darkness came a terrible howl. The near sheep hurried toward the center of the flock, where their fellows were thickest. Smitty's horse shuddered, and Smitty—who'd often heard that howl before—couldn't repress the nasty little shiver that walked down his spine. The wounded wolf snarled, and the Kid fired a third time. He must have missed, because the snarling and screaming went on—it seemed forever—as the hurt animal withdrew.

The Kid's lips were drawn back in a snarl, and his leveled Dragoon was rock steady as he peered into the darkness. Silently, Smitty kneed his horse away. . . .

Smitty wondered why he liked the Kid. He wasn't anymore account than Muleshoe's other riders. When Smitty and the foreman had ridden into Soda Springs looking for men, they were the wrong outfit in the wrong season. The few decent punchers who might work for a sheep outfit were looking for work with a more permanent flavor to it. When snow hung in the air, men looked for jobs where they could hole up until spring, not work that'd leave them hungry just when the weather turned.

Renfrew had taken what he could—and the Kid, with no experience whatsoever, wasn't the best of the lot.

One day in Soda Springs, three days on the trail, four days to gather the woolies out of the draws and brambles where they'd grazed all summer. So far, it was taking a whole lot longer than Renfrew had estimated, and he wasn't slow to blame it on his men.

The foreman was a handsome young man with a horseman's narrow hips and a roper's shoulders. He wore his blond hair short, combed to one side with a part straight as a ruler. His blue eyes were big and often worried. He never drank and spoke sarcastically of those who did. He always had a wet brown quirly hanging on his lip. His daddy had been a rider, and his mother—well, she was no better than she should be. He thought he was in love with Mary Anne Murchison, though he probably confused love with ambition.

He thought about her often. When old J.D. went to

his reward, maybe he could persuade Miss Murchison to sell these pesky woolies and buy some *real* livestock again.

Renfrew's riders were too low in the social scheme to be blind or ignorant, and every one of them had noticed that the woolies moved along better when the rider's pressure was steady and slow. Cows you could push along pretty fast and let them graze at night. If these woolies didn't snatch a bite every now and again they got restive. Muleshoe's Bums had learned to ride slow and steady behind their charges, though Renfrew exhorted them constantly to move faster. "You think we got months to get these bastards down to warmer country?" he yelled. "You think we're gonna pay you gents for screwing around?" They'd push harder until the sheep balked or until Renfrew rode on to the next hapless rider with his harangue.

"Man's a fool, Kid." That was Smitty's considered opinion, and the Kid shared it because whatever Smith said had to be true. It was Smitty who'd shown him the road agent's spin—the little trick that killed Morgan Earp in a Tombstone alleyway.

Smith showed him all the spins and dips the gunfighters used to supple their hands. Every evening, once the sheep were bedded down, the Kid put in an hour of practice beyond the firelight, where nobody could mock him. For the first three days his hands had hurt, the heavy pistol twisting and banging his knuckles, but now they hardly hurt at all.

Smith rode impassively, spitting a stream of tobacco juice from time to time. Smith had pale eyes and a gimp, which the Kid presumed was an old bullet wound, and Smith never told him different.

Though some found it hard to believe, the old belly robber had ridden with Quantrill because even the fiercest owlhoots need a camp cook. Smitty's full name was Charles Smithson, and that was how it read on the wanted posters where he figured. He'd known some of the great gunfighters and had actually ridden with them—tending to his bacon and beans, his blue enamel pot of coffee and fatback and pemmican—when they were running so hard he couldn't keep a fire going. Smith had known the greats and been just as fascinated by these men as the Kid was now when Smitty repeated the legends around the campfire at night.

The Kid imagined Smitty had had a bigger part in the events he described than he let on. Smith thought it was a harmless deception. He'd known the James boys, hadn't he? That was God's own truth. If the Kid thought he'd ridden beside Jesse and Frank when guns were blazing, that was his problem.

By Smith's Ingersoll it was close to eleven-thirty, and men who breakfast before sunrise have a pretty good appetite when the sun's high in the sky. That creek over there, looked like the water was okay, and it was upstream from the good meadow where the woolies could graze. Smith stood on the wagon seat and waved his sombrero until Renfrew rode over. "I'll be wanting to dish up some grub," he said.

"Jesus! Already?"

"It's a good place to stop."

"Naw. Let's put a few more miles behind us."

It got to be noon and then an hour past noon. By

the time Renfrew finally called a halt everybody was so damn hungry their bellies were sucked up against their backbones, and men that hungry get snappish and unpleasant with each other. Since there was no nearby stream, the coffee was boiled from the stale cask water, and there wasn't enough extra so a man could daub the dust off his face before he sat down with his tin plate and cup. Biscuits, beans, and brown gravy. Black coffee. A man could get a little sweetener for his coffee if he asked polite enough.

The Kid propped his boot heel on the spokes of the chuck-wagon wheel. He tilted his wide-brimmed hat down over his eyes and put away a second helping without much trouble. Since the Kid thought of Smitty as a gunfighter, he never mentioned the cooking, never said it was good or bad. The Kid didn't know Smitty the belly robber; Smitty the gunslinger was his pal.

It puzzled Smitty. He was a pretty good trail cook and proud of the products of his Dutch oven. He got compliments from everybody except Renfrew and the Kid. Puzzling.

The Kid's hat was a Stetson look-alike. Low-grade cotton felt with no beaver in it, and no matter how he shaped the brim, it drooped at the edges and wouldn't hold a crease. Against the mountain wall a hawk was climbing. The Kid could hear a bunch of crows hollering, threatening the hawk from below. Crows can gang up on a hawk and kill it, but the Kid would never know that because it didn't fit his image of the world. He thought he was like that hawk; high and lonely, dangerous, a hunter. He readjusted the brim of his hat, lower on his forehead. It drooped.

Since the sheep had no grass to graze on in the rocky defile Renfrew had selected as a lunch stop, they walked around aimlessly and came in close to the chuck wagon to watch the humans going about their strange lives. Sheep smell bad.

Renfrew gulped his coffee, though it was so hot the lip of the tin cup hurt his lips. After everybody had one cup of Joe and one smoke they'd mount up again.

The Kid was standing around like a gunfighter, the three breeds were laughing and joking, the Spaniards ate quietly, and Fat Matthews was starting on his fourth helping of beans. For social comment, he cut a loud fart.

"Christ," Smitty said. "You smell worse'n them woolies do."

For answer, Fat Matthews lifted one haunch and commented again.

On a cattle drive in rough country a puncher could expect to change horses at least twice a day and maybe three times if he caught the nighthawk duty. Pushing sheep was easier on the horses, and you could ride the same animal from dawn to dusk if you had a mind to. Renfrew changed his saddle to a fresh quarter horse just for something to do while the Bums finished eating.

Forty minutes after Renfrew signaled a halt they were on the move again, pushing the woolies through the defile. On the other side it opened into a broad high valley; more rocks than grass, more sagebrush than rocks, and more mesquite than sagebrush.

The sheep tugged at the tough brush as they passed. Renfrew had heard that damn sheep could eat anything.

It was ironic. Probably he owed his job to the sheep—he'd been an ordinary puncher till all the others handed J.D. Murchison their walking papers. He was tied to these stupid animals, and he'd bear the stigma among decent punchers forever. He wiped his forehead. Couple dots toward the mouth of the valley. No, three, four of them. Mule deer? Couldn't be woods buffalo up this high so late in the season. Riders.

The Kid was standing up in his stirrups. One of the half-breeds waved to another; they knew some fragments of the sign language that served all the Indians as a universal tongue. The half-breed's fingers were busy as worms.

Hunting party? Prospectors? Maybe an army patrol looking for Bannacks. The Bannacks had been peaceful Indians until whites discovered the good graze on Camas Prairie. The Bannacks used camas root as a staple. They made meal and flour out of it. They weren't happy when the white man's cattle and sheep started eating food that had fed them for God knows how far back in misty history. A long time. The Bannacks shot a couple of drovers and the army came out against the Bannacks. So far the army had had the best of it.

The Nez Percé still held their land, their horses, their herds of domestic cattle, their sawmills and flour mills. Under Chief Joseph they were a friendly and prosperous people. Jack Renfrew thought they were a bunch of damn redskins and the sooner they were put on reservations, the sooner whites would sleep easy at night. His was a common opinion at that time.

The dots became a loose line of riders growing a bit larger but still a good distance away. No pack animals, so they weren't prospectors. Maybe they were punchers looking for strays. Murchison's sheep weren't the only animals to use the Owyhee Trail from the high country down to the prairie. There was plenty of cattle sign. All the good cooking wood had been cut near the best campsites. It wasn't a big problem for Renfrew, since he never camped at the best campsites.

Renfrew moved up to the point. The Kid was there before him, up in his stirrups again. "It's awful late for travelers," he said with a growl in his voice.

"Probably looking for strays. This trail goes down the other side of the mountains all the way to Jackson Hole."

"Uh-huh."

Four men, on four huge horses, rode up.

In the lead was Teton Jackson, who wore an elkhide jacket with long fringe dangling from the sleeves. The jacket glowed like it had been dipped in tallow. Splotches on his right sleeve where, six months ago, he'd butchered something. Scorch marks on the cuffs where he'd come too close to the fire.

His flat black hat had an eagle tail feather tucked in the broad, moldy green band. He wore a string of grizzly claws around his neck. His beard was black and slicked down with bear grease. He'd lost four teeth in a fight, and the gap was dead center. He was smiling now.

With him were Red Smart, Con Hennessey, and a yonger gent Renfrew knew only as Butch. The four men carried long guns across their saddlebows. Teton Jackson's .44 Henry was decorated Indian-style with rows of brass studs outlining the butt plate and medicine feathers dangling from the muzzle.

Red Smart was a pale, pale man with red hair the color of arterial blood. His eyes were pale too, as colorless as the rest of his body. He wore chaps and the flannel jacket of a working puncher and carried two Colts, cross-draw, in a saddle holster. Most of the cows he'd worked in his short life had been the other man's.

Con Hennessey was a big man who wore a boiler-plate black suit that had been new once—though it was hard to guess when. The bowler hat on his huge head was a couple of sizes too small, which somewhat ruined the effect. In blatant emulation of Teton Jackson, he wore an eagle tail feather poked into his hatband. His black suit coat was buttoned up. No pistols in sight, but he handled the sawed-off Greener with one hand like maybe that's all it was—a big pistol.

The sheep flowed by the riders like they were boulders in a stream. *Baa*'s. Bleats.

Renfrew's quirly picked that moment to disintegrate, and he picked the soggy mess off his lip. He knew these men.

Teton Jackson spat a stream of juice onto a sheep's topknot. Red Smart crinkled his nose. "Stinks," he opined.

Teton Jackson and his gang of badhats lived south of here, at a scrubby roadhouse Teton called Jackson's and honest citizens called Robber's Roost.

If you wanted to take a herd of cows across the mountains into Wyoming, Teton was your man. And there were plenty of Wyoming buyers who didn't scrutinize a brand or inspect an ear notch so long as the price was right. Nobody knew how he moved them so silently, and nobody ever saw his bunch with cows. But he sure never seemed to hurt for money, and he sure didn't do a lick of work.

"What's it take to kill one of these things?" he asked. His voice was as rough as a prospector's pan before you get the big pebbles out of it.

Renfrew kept his face neutral. Blank. "Oh, they'll die same as anything else," he said. Then: "I didn't know you had business up this way."

If you were going to take a wagon into the mountains (or so it was said) with just you and your wife and young'uns, well then, you hoped like the devil that Jackson's bunch didn't get wind of it. Folks said that those small family wagons just vanished off the face of the earth—man, woman, and child. They said that Teton Jackson might know more than he was saying.

Ignoring Renfrew's question, the bearded man said, "That's a relief. I was afraid the fuckers were immortal. Hell, if they'll die when you put lead into 'em, we cowboys got nothing to worry about."

A chill struck Renfrew's bowels. He shifted in his saddle. He licked his lips. "These are Muleshoe animals," he said, and his voice was almost as dispassionate as Jackson's own.

Jackson lifted his hat, inspected the lining, and scratched his head vigorously. He squished something between his fingertips and smeared it on his saddle horn. "Naw," he said. "Every Muleshoe animal I ever seen had a brand on it." He grinned. His eyes were not amused. "The Muleshoe brand. Hell of a thing to alter—if a man had a mind to. Oh, you can burn an R into the hide and call it the Rocking R, but it'll always look like a Muleshoe that's been altered. Hell of a brand."

"Sheep don't need brands," Renfrew said. He laughed. He laughed alone. "Hell, who'd want to rustle a sheep?"

"You callin' us rustlers?" Jackson asked, politely.

"Oh, hell no! Hell no! Why'd I go and say a thing like that?"

"Boys," Jackson said to his gang, "Murchison's foreman here, he don't think we're rustlers. Ain't that nice?"

Red Smart said it was. He spoke with a lisp.

"I suppose you don't mind if we ride along," Jackson said. "Me and the boys are scared of Indians." He said that deadpan, but this time his eyes were laughing.

Well, Jack Renfrew couldn't think of any real objection and didn't feel like mentioning that Jackson's men had come from the opposite direction and would be retracing their footsteps. "Sure. Glad to have a white man's company," Renfrew allowed, wishing he could swallow his words.

Teton Jackson smiled quite brilliantly, and Red Smart smiled too. The smiles didn't reassure Renfrew.

"Well, we'll just help you out some," Jackson said.

"Yeah. Help you out." Red Smart whispered.

"Fine. That'll be fine."

After the riders had entered the big flock, the Kid rode up close—stirrup to stirrup—and said, "Maybe it ain't my place to be saying anything, but Christ, man, those hombres are up to no good."

"When I want your opinion I'll ask it."

Renfrew rode point. Jackson and his men stayed in the drag. One rode with the half-breeds, Red Smart palled around with the Spaniards, and Butch discovered a new affection for Fat Matthews.

It got dark early, and despite Renfrew's desire to get miles, they pulled up by a spring to make camp. It was a silent crew that lined up for Smith's good grub. Teton Jackson and his men lined up with the rest, joking and griping about the food. "Christ, you poor sons of bitches eat this swill?"

The elk steaks were burned black, and the biscuits were as big around as a tin cup, just like most punchers liked them. The coffee was black as hell and strong enough to float bar steel, just like most punchers wanted it. Smitty bristled but held his tongue.

The half-breeds struck up an acquaintance with Jackson and his men, but the Kid stayed on the other side of the fire—just as far away as he could get. Smitty hunkered beside the Kid, staring at Jackson through the steam that came off his cup.

"That sonofabitch," the Kid breathed.

"He's bad medicine, that one," the old man said. "Him and that Red Smart took on a posse last year. Outside of Webster. A dozen men rode out with that posse, but no more'n six limped back home again."

"He ain't half the man Cole Younger is. Or Wesley Hardin, neither."

"No he ain't. But he ain't no baby lamb with fleece white as driven snow. He's generally got twenty men riding with him. There's some rougher men than his bunch, but you'd go a far piece to find them."

"What do they want?"

A shrug. "I dunno. They use this trail sometimes, or so I heard. Maybe this is one of the times. Maybe they got a dozen of their partners back in the woods where they'll come out a little later and take those sheep for their own."

"Oh yeah?" The Kid was as defiant as the young hawk he compared himself to. Teton Jackson spotted his angry glare and walked over. Jackson wore dirty stovepipe-gray pants with narrow black stripes. The Kid's eyes were on a level with Jackson's knees. Jackson wore his Colt army-fashion—high on his waist in the flap-covered holster that protected the weapon from weather. He never set down his Henry. The Henry came in a variety of lengths, from hunting rifle to saddle carbine, and Teton Jackson's was the shortest. He held it easily with his hand curled under the lever and his finger inside the trigger guard. He looked at the Kid, who returned his examination with interest.

"Well, I'm damned," Jackson said, mildly amused. Then he went and hunkered back down on the other side of the fire. Though he'd bitched about Smitty's food, he took his tin plate back for another serving of beans. He gnawed a second elk steak in his fist. The other fist held his Henry.

Jackson tossed his bone into the campfire. He spooned up the last of his beans and tossed the plate in the fire too. Smitty jumped to his feet. If it had been one of the Muleshoe hands it would have been hell to pay. He said nothing. He retrieved the plate.

The Kid's jaw dropped.

"Well, I thank you boys for your hospitality," Jackson said. The front sight of his Henry lifted and scratched his cheekbone. Con Hennessey came over beside him. Con's suit jacket was so tight across his middle that the buttonholes gaped with strain. He licked bean grease off his cheek. The Greener hung in his hand. His eyes were round and bulbous. Outrage or innocent surprise.

The gunman they knew as Butch stood behind the fire where the Muleshoe punchers were sitting, coffee cups in their hands or partway through rolling a quirly.

Red Smart was gone. Couldn't see him anywhere.

Teton Jackson worked his tongue around his mouth and sucked until he got that last bit of meat.

Jack Renfrew rose to his feet real unhappily. He was a ranch foreman—he was no gunfighter.

"I don't suppose any of you boys seen a cow," Jackson said vaguely.

"No, no," Renfrew replied. "We haven't seen any kind of a cow up here." Renfrew was real pleased these boys were hunting a stray animal—their other possible motives were so much worse.

"You sure?" Teton Jackson stuck out his rifle muzzle like he was measuring an animal. " 'Bout that tall. Maybe half again as long as that. Four feet. Tail. Some of 'em got horns."

"Well, I'm sorry you got a stray cow," Renfrew said. "We'll keep our eyes peeled."

"I guess you wouldn't know what a cow looks like," Jackson said. He turned and winked at Butch, who leaned over and whispered something in one half-breed's ear. The ripple passed down the lineup of men. Butch stood with his arms crossed. His hands were very close to the guns he wore.

The half-breed reached into his holster, took out his pistol, and threw it into the dust in front of his feet. He grunted. He warmed his icy hands with his coffee cup.

The next breed tossed a rifle out there. His companion shook his head furiously side to side and wouldn't meet anyone's eyes.

Snick, snick, snick. The sound of Butch's Colt going to full cock was unmistakable.

The half-breed turned his desperate face. "I ain't got no iron," he whined. Anxiously his hand went to his sheath knife. He tossed that into the dirt to show good faith.

Some Spanish jabber. The old Spaniard carried a gambler's derringer, of all things; that and his son's knife clattered on the growing pile of weapons.

Teton Jackson watched with neutral eyes. "I don't know if a man deserves to be called a cowman when he don't know what a cow looks like." When the last of the guns were in the pile he faced Renfrew and said, "I don't suppose it was an honest mistake you made about those cows."

"What mistake?"

Teton Jackson chuckled expansively. "I know you're

honest punchers, and I hate to break the news to you.''

''What news?''

''Boys, I know you been thinkin' you came up here to pick up a herd of cows and bring 'em down to the Camas Prairie. Nothin' wrong with that. Every year somebody runs cows over this trail. Hell,'' he laughed, ''we've been known to do it.'' The big man in the boiler-plate suit laughed. The man who was known as Butch laughed too. One of the half-breeds giggled.

''It was a mistake anybody could have made, boys. I got to tell you, those critters you been eatin' the dust of, they ain't cows, not cows at all. They're sheep, that's what they are.''

The Kid had had enough. He got to his feet and glowered at Teton Jackson, which wasn't as effective as it might have been had he been a foot or so taller. His fake Stetson flapped dangerously. With a deliberate motion he unfastened the leather thong that kept his Dragoon from bouncing out of his holster.

Smitty got up beside him.

'' 'Course they're sheep,'' the Kid said. ''Any damn fool can see that.''

Mock puzzlement. ''You mean you knew they was sheep all along? Aaaaaah. Damn, I thought you boys had made a little mistake. I didn't think any of you was shit-lickin' mother-humpin' sheepmen.'' Jackson's Henry trembled. The Kid's hand formed a claw above the butt of his Dragoon and the sweat stood out on his upper lip. Couldn't see his eyes under all that hat.

Big Con Hennessey moved over a mite where he'd
have a clean shot.

"I was hopin' once you boys realized your mistake, you'd just ride on down the trail and leave these
fuckin' woolies right here."

The Kid stepped sideways, away from the old
man, giving them both room.

Jackson's voice was dead calm. "Renfrew, you
dealin' yourself in?" Jackson went into a crouch.

Renfrew showed his hands in the air. "Oh no," he
said. "I ain't no gunslinger. Never pretended to
be." His hands were safe in the air.

"Smitty? You sittin' in?" Jackson's voice was
hoarse with triumph.

The old man seemed to shrink inside his clothes.
Visibly, he lost life. "I never carried iron in my life.
Everybody knows that." He turned to the boy, "Kid,
this ain't the place or the time. Don't give them an
excuse to kill you."

The boy turned his head so fast his loose hat
stayed in place so it was facing forward while he was
facing sideways. He grabbed the damn thing and
hurled it to the ground. His forehead was pale where
the hat had protected him from the sun. "Smitty, you
rode with Quantrill. These here are just two-bit cow
thieves. Jesus, Smitty!" You could almost hear the
tears in his voice.

The shot was very sudden, very loud. The bullet
took the Kid in the small of the back.

His mouth flew wide open, like he was trying to
vent the agony. He clapped both hands over his
spine, arched, and stepped stiff-legged forward, el-

bows locked, mouth jammed open, big-eyed as a hammered calf.

When he flopped into the campfire, his knees stayed bent and his back was arched and he rocked on the fire with his belly. He died.

Smitty jerked the Kid out of the flames. His shirt hadn't even had time to catch on fire.

Red Smart came out of the darkness, holstering his long-barreled Remington. "Damn. I hate for a man to call me a two-bit cow thief," he said. "I never worked for less than four bits in my life. And," he concluded triumphantly, "that was for friends."

2

Muleshoe headquarters lay in the opening of a wooded canyon. The spring that watered the house created a couple of good stock tanks before sparkling its way into the hayfields. The hayfields, where the sheep were confined once the snow fell, served as good graze this time of the year. A couple of men could guard the sheep against predators and keep them fed. When Muleshoe was a cattle ranch the punchers spent the winter mending equipment and fence—and feeding cows is a much bigger job than feeding sheep, because a good cow eats five times what'll feed a ewe.

J.D. Murchison thought he'd keep Renfrew and maybe that pal of Smitty's—"Kid Somebody."

"Daddy, would you like another cup of tea?"

"Don't suppose you could lace it with a little of that rye whiskey in the kitchen cupboard."

"Daddy, you know what the doctor said—no drinking, no hard riding, plenty of rest, no excitement of any kind whatsoever."

"I was there. I heard."

She brought his tea and set it down on the porch railing. From where he sat he could see the hayfields that explained so much of the Muleshoe's power.

24

Man who could raise enough hay in the mountain country could pretty well do whatever with livestock he wanted. J.D.'s hands were icy cold, and he pushed them under the folds of the lap robe.

The wall at his back was made of heavy logs on a laid stone foundation. A couple of Italian masons he hired away from the Denver Rio Grande crew. Didn't speak twenty words of English between them, but the stone they laid looked seamless, and the keystone arch of the fireplace in the living room was eight feet across if it was an inch. The logs were Douglas fir from the high country, and each log had a girth of thirty inches.

When an active man gets dropped to his knees by a bum heart before he turns fifty, that man has had all the surprise he needs. J.D.'d always been up with the sun, and sometimes he was still working when the last faint bars of the sunset faded in the western sky. He was a rough man; he hoped he was a fair one. The old-timers in the territory counted him among the salt of the earth. The newcomers seemed to like spicier foods. He supposed it was ever thus. When he and his cattleman pals crossed the Rockies they'd dislodged the mountain men—who'd dislodged the Indians before them. No telling who the Indians had dislodged.

There was still a little green in the fields. He'd planted a little rye in some fields, and rye would continue to make growth until a hard frost. Two, three weeks and he'd wake up one morning and come out here to see a white glaze clinging to all the grass, creating tiny sculptures from the tussocks. He sighed. He rubbed his right leg, which was going to sleep.

He shouldn't complain. Anybody who'd seen one western morning out here, with the sky stretching like a taut second skin above the planet, like it was almost too much for itself to contain, with the silent mountains a hundred miles away and the awesome expanse of the buffalo grass—hell, anybody who'd seen just one morning like that didn't really have any complaints.

His tea was cold. He hadn't wanted it anyway.

His hair was coal black, his eyebrows bushy and just as black. His eyes didn't seem to move so much as other men's. They had a habit of fixing on what they were looking at and holding it until inspection was complete. He was bandy-legged and big-chested, and ropes of useless muscle hung from his arms like a sad history.

He wished he had a son. In his whole life—and he'd made the customary number of grievous mistakes; maybe more than his share—that was his sole regret. Mary Anne was his daughter, and he loved her. But he wished he'd had a son to carry on when he crossed into the shadowland. Funny, he'd come to think of dying like the Indians did. One day he expected to find himself in the shadowland. The white man's heaven (or hell) would have surprised him. He snorted. *I've lived in this country too long,* he thought.

A son could hold the Muleshoe. Times were tight, and plenty of big cattle outfits had gone under the hammer. The price of silver had collapsed—and much of the ready money in this part of the West came out of those silver mines.

Funny thing about hard times. The only thing that

can reconcile you to your hard times is the other
man's worse times.

Maybe he should have held on to the cows. By this
time next fall anybody with cows would be in fine
shape. The cattle cycle would start right up again,
and all the boosters would come out of the wood-
work, and pretty soon every cattleman would think
he was due to become a millionaire.

He wished he'd be around to see it. Muleshoe had
plenty of feed for eight thousand sheep. Hayricks
dotted the fields like beehives. Man could take that
extra hay and buy up a thousand cows for a dime on
the dollar late in the winter when everybody else was
running out of feed. No cattleman will starve an
animal if he can sell.

It was going to be a long, hard winter, too. After
thirty years in this country, Murchison knew. The
first frost had come on September 4, for God's sake.
The signs were everywhere: the wooliebears were
wide-banded, and all the geese and ducks who should
have been migrating now were long gone.

Murchison had always taken a certain savage pleasure in getting a little bit more out of this hard land
than the next man could. When the hunters came to
hunt Muleshoe land, Murchison said no. No other
ranch owner gave a damn, so his attitude was thought
peculiar but not particularly inconvenient. When the
best hunting was finished on the other man's range,
Murchison advertised back east: "Hunt Wild Game
amongst Pristine Beauty (Easiest Connections via
Oregon Short Line)." And the tenderfeet had come
every summer to hunt Muleshoe's deer, elk, buffalo,

bear, and moose. It had made a few precious dollars for the ranch.

While other men were clinging desperately to their cattle, Murchison quietly unloaded every single longhorn he possessed. Sold the bulk of them to the scion of a California gold fortune. Young man fancied himself a cattle baron. Murchison snorted. He'd be broke just as soon as the rest, but he had paid J.D. Murchison top dollar.

His eight thousand woolies were already worth half again what he'd paid for them. Egyptian cotton had failed this year, and mysterious troubles in China had hurt silk production, so wool was a premium fabric. Come spring shearing, it would be pure gold.

Pity he wouldn't see it. He coughed into his hand and looked at the wetness his spittle had made, just like he was some lunger worried about blood spots. His lungs were fine. He closed his hand and squeezed it until it hurt. Damn, he wanted to live a little bit longer. Mary Anne would sell the sheep off as soon as they were sheared and get back into cattle. She wouldn't be able to read the signs—those guideposts in the muddy river that told her father when to row and when to just drift along.

He heard his daughter upstairs humming a dance tune. Too bad about ranch life. A pretty girl didn't get much chance for the kind of fun she'd had when she was back east at that fancy school. The next ranch was fifty miles south, and ordinary ranch hands weren't fit dancing partners for a woman like Mary Anne who'd grown up with every advantage. *Except*, he thought, *a long-lived father*.

He sighed. He crossed his leg the opposite way

and rubbed that leg because it was numb too. If he stood without first rubbing his legs there was no feeling in them at all, and he'd just topple over like a collapsed doll.

This damn heart thing had come on so fast. Four months ago he hadn't dreamt anything was wrong. Oh, he'd get dizzy now and again for no reason, and sometimes he wouldn't be able to hold down his grub on a hot day, but he surely hadn't expected to die.

So be it. Mary Anne Murchison couldn't handle the Muleshoe without a man; that was as plain as the nose on your face. He'd have to find somebody suitable. His foreman, Renfrew, behaved like a simpering idiot every time he was in the same room with Mary Anne, and J.D. could have married them off, but Renfrew was as dense as a post.

The barn swallows were swooping over the fields. Swoops and swirls of birds coming from the horse barns where they nested.

Why him? Hell, there were plenty of men just loafed away their whole lives, wasted their days in sleep and their nights in drink, and they'd be going on, half oblivious, long after he was under the ground. Damn!

He'd be glad when the first woolies came into the lots—by his calculations that couldn't be much before tomorrow, but he was waiting anyway. He didn't have much better to do.

His daughter was happy with the new gown that had been delivered out to the ranch yesterday. The gowns were pictured in *Harper's Bazaar* or *Leslie's Magazine* and copied by Mary Anne's seamstress. Sometimes the results were satisfactory.

Maybe if he sent her off the ranch for the winter, down to Boise maybe. Bennett, the territorial governor, had a son, Jim. Old Bennett was famous for his drinking habits; Murchison had heard the boy was the same way. Old man Bennett used to go into the bars and holler, "Is there one sonofabitch in this bar who'll have a drink with the territorial governor?"

J.D. needed more time to marry his daughter off—time to protect Muleshoe. If he'd only had a little warning he could have set this thing up right, but he doubted he'd see the crocuses in the spring. From the topside.

He grinned. It hurt.

He'd fire Renfrew's crew after they had the sheep lotted up. No sense carrying dead weight through the cold time. It'd be him and Renfrew and the Kid and Smitty. Smitty played cribbage. J.D. had never asked Renfrew what he did in his spare time. He hoped he wasn't one of those men who cleaned his clothes, sewed, and read gospel tracts. That'd be poor company for his last days on earth.

The riders came into view at a trot. Six, eight—looked like the whole damn crew. J.D. Murchison came up supporting himself on the porch rail. Where in hell were his animals?

Generally one rider would come on ahead to open the gates. But all of them? What the hell?

"Mary Anne, get down here."

Her light footfall. Mary Anne Murchison stepped onto the porch—a woman in the prime of her life. She was slightly frail—bigger-bosomed than most but skinny in the hindquarters. Her hair was as gold as new oats, and her eyes were cornflower blue.

The two watched silently as the riders drew nearer and nearer.

"There's somebody missing, Papa."

"No he ain't. He's what's stretched across that pack animal. That's a dead man tied to that horse."

Renfrew was up front, looking neither to left nor right. The others moped along behind. Even the horses seemed to share low spirits.

Smitty swung around back. The chuck wagon went directly to the storeroom beside the kitchen, and Smitty started humping his provisions back into storage.

"Renfrew?"

"Yes, sir. Your sheep, they . . . well, they aren't here."

"Noticed that, m'boy. You better have a real good idea where they are."

Renfrew stayed on his horse but took his hat off. The other riders busied themselves loosening cinches and laying their stirrups up on the saddles.

"I believe they're in that high meadow, just the other side of Two Medicine Creek. They was there when we left 'em."

"I see." Murchison's hands had gone white. He deliberately relaxed. Deliberately, he made himself breathe slow and easy. He could feel his heart leaping around inside him like some kind of trapped animal.

"Daughter, you take my arm. Renfrew, come inside and tell me why my animals are still in the mountains when any damn fool can see it's gonna be winter up there in a week, and when it snows they'll all damn well die."

Inside, J.D. Murchison settled into one of those

newfangled morris chairs. It was nice to have a chair
you could adjust so many different ways, though
none of those adjustments was particularly comfortable. Renfrew worked the brim of his Stetson around
and around in his hands.

"Well?" Murchison croaked.

Renfrew told his boss about Teton Jackson's play.
He described the Kid's death. "It was awful," he
said. "The way they killed him. Like you'd stamp a
damn bug!"

Murchison looked his question.

Renfrew blushed. "There was four of them," he
said. "And no tellin' how many more of his men
within earshot. I didn't figure that one to show all his
cards at once, no sir!" Renfrew seemed to take pride
in Teton Jackson's cunning.

"You know where they come from. They got that
old stage station, Robber's Roost. No tellin' how
many in Jackson's gang or how many he had out in
the darkness. Mr. Murchison, I never hired on for no
gunfighter! You want your livestock moved, even
sheep, why then, I'm your boy. But when it comes to
gunplay—"

"Shut your mouth." Murchison's fingers drummed
on the wooden arm of his chair. "Now, daughter.
You'll not begrudge me a small glass of whiskey?"

"Dad?"

"Get it." As she went to the corner cupboard for
his glass, Murchison eyed Renfrew. Renfrew eyed
his hat.

"Did they steal the sheep?"

"No, sir. They just told us to leave them. Teton

Jackson, he's a real cowman, and he just plain took offense—''

"Bullshit! Boy, you get a few more years behind you and if you don't stay a fool, you'll know the only reason cowmen hate sheep is because they ain't got anything more conveient to hate. If they didn't have sheep to hate, they'd hate the damn wolves or the coyotes. Man out in this country just don't feel quite right without some kind of natural enemy, and those sheep will do until something better comes along. That don't mean a man'd kill because of it."

"Teton Jackson said all the sheep would stay in that high plain until they was bones, every one of them. That's what he said."

"He just couldn't stand to be on the same planet with my eight thousand sheep? Bullshit."

His reluctant daughter handed him whiskey. It was a smaller glass than usual, and it was only half full. When he tossed it back, spots of color flowered in his cheeks. He swallowed again, convulsively, and his eyes bulged. He paused until his breathing was good before he said, "Man like Teton Jackson never was no idealist. If he wants my livestock dead, there's money in it for him, that's sure. The Kid fought back, you say?"

Smitty's voice came from behind them. "Yes, sir," he said. "The Wolf Kid fought back. It wasn't no fair play, neither. They gunned him from ambush. Goddamn backshooters!"

"Come around where I can see you, Smitty!" Murchison snapped. He had no patience for screwing himself around to listen to the other man.

Smitty was rarely seen without his short cook's

apron. Tightly buckled around his waist was a brown steel revolver with a plain ebony butt. "It's a J.W. Dance," Smitty said. "It was issue during the war."

"And why are you wearing it?" Murchison demanded.

"Maybe if I'd been wearing it, the Wolf Kid would still be alive."

"The Wolf Kid?"

"That was what he always wanted to be called, and if you can't honor a dead man's wish, what can you honor?" Smitty folded his arms, looking self-righteous.

Renfrew said, "We never had a chance."

"I'd say my flock of eight thousand sheep never had a chance. Jesus Christ, man. Do you know what I stand to lose if those woolies stay up there and starve to death?"

Renfrew shook his head.

"Every damn penny I own and some of what I borrowed is up there in that damn canyon. I suggest we commence to figuring how to bring them down."

His daughter hovered. "Daddy, don't get excited!"

He swallowed his irritation. He created a strange little smile and he said, "I . . . am . . . not . . . excited. Take the cashbox, dear, and pay off the men. They were supposed to draw a dollar a day and food. Eight days. Pay 'em four dollars each. Tell 'em the rest of their wages got left in the mountains with the damn sheep."

She took the leather-covered cashbox outside. One of the punchers looked at the four silver cartwheels in his hand. He jiggled them. He said, "It's gonna be a hard winter, ma'am."

Mary Anne smiled her pretty smile at him. "Perhaps you should ride south for the winter."

"Ain't got no horse." The man shouldered his saddle and marched off toward town. Last time he'd ever work for a Murchison.

They made two short files on either side of the Muleshoe road, keeping their distance from one another because nobody wanted to talk. One of the half-breeds was kicking a stone, and that was the last Mary Anne saw of them—that breed booting a stone across the indifferent landscape.

When she stepped back into the ranchhouse she was glad to be back with people she understood. Papa was a gentleman, and Renfrew was working his way to being a gentleman, and she'd known old Smitty since he first came into this country and started cooking for them. He was a good cook too, rare in this country, and could turn out a first-rate apple pie or a buffalo roast on her papa's birthday when they had everybody over to the Muleshoe and the rafters rang with laughter and song.

Mary Anne sighed.

J.D. Murchison was saying they shouldn't cry over spilt milk. "And that means you too, Renfrew. Just so long as it don't happen again. I'm too far along in my life to go breakin' in any new foreman, so this time we'll just overlook what you done."

Renfrew's face was puckered like he'd swallowed a bitter hickory nut. He wanted to object, wanted to make his excuses, but Murchison wasn't leaving him any room.

"We ain't gonna be able to lick this Teton Jackson

by ourselves. He's a rustler, some kind of curly wolf, and he's got curly wolves for pals.''

Smitty made a face. "They ain't worth two bits," he said. "The Wolf Kid was right. They're a bunch of mean bastards who know how to use their Colts, but you put 'em up against a real hardcase . . .''

"They're devils," Renfrew said, still smarting from the tongue-lashing he'd gotten. "Teton Jackson, Red Smart, and all those murderers. They'd kill you soon as say how-de-do.''

"Smitty!" And there was something in old Murchison's voice that held them all. "I want the truth from you now.''

Old Smitty kind of straightened up and said, "Yes, sir.''

"Ever since I knowed you, you were always running on about the Quantrill guerrillas, the James boys . . .''

"Yes, sir.''

"Well?''

Long pause. Smitty said, "I rode with Quantrill, like I said. I never killed nobody. I was the camp cook.''

Murchison grunted, not happily. He said they needed some tough riders of their own to get the sheep down to the home ranch.

His daughter said she and Renfrew would go into Soda Springs as soon as they got their horses hitched.

Renfrew seconded that motion.

"And what the hell are you gonna find in Soda Springs?" said Murchison. "Won't be anybody except the men we just fired, drinking their troubles away and burning for a chance to insult you. If there was any good men for hire in Soda Springs, we would have hired 'em long ago.''

"John Slocum," Smitty said.

Murchison was too heated to pay any particular attention. He ordered another drink from his daughter, just like he had a perfect right to drink whiskey. The glass she brought was a better draught than the first one, and it seemed quite natural to bring whiskey to a man who'd been a teetotaler since spring. "If them boys are devils, we'll just have to hire our own devil," he said. "Better the devil you know—"

"John Slocum." Patiently, Smitty repeated the name.

Murchison looked puzzled.

"Slocum's in Idaho," Smitty said. "I heard that he was. He never got himself on a handbill like the rest of the boys, so a man hears of him from time to time. I heard he was working over at Silver City."

Murchison shook his head. "Who the hell . . . ?"

"Oh, he's your devil, Mr. Murchison. He can work the Colt revolver with either hand or both, though he favors his right. He's terrible good with a rifle and can ride a strong fast horse to death. I heard he's honest.''

"Silver City's halfway across the state," Murchison objected.

"If we leave early in the morning, take the train in Soda Springs, we'll be in Silver City by dark," Renfrew said, grateful that something fell within his own expertise. He liked the solution: Hire a tough nut to crack the other tough nuts while honest cattle . . . sheepmen like himself went about their business. Made sense to him.

"It's a lot of trouble for one damn gunslinger."

"I've seen him, Mr. Murchison. I stood across a campfire from John Slocum many a time. I know him. He'll make Teton Jackson eat crow."

A tiny bit of genuine curiosity flared behind Murchison's sick eyes.

Without asking permission, Smitty poured himself a shot of the boss's private stock to wet his whistle.

In the first years of the war Smitty had owned a small inn, the Elkhorn Tavern, down in Arkansas. Wife, two daughters, and a son who'd gone off to fight for the Confederacy. Arkansas wasn't as dangerous as Kansas, but just because fewer got killed by the jawhawkers in Arkansas didn't mean you were any less dead.

Smitty had been away hunting a couple of runaway horses. When he rode back to the Elkhorn it was broken chimneys and the roof was caved into the burnt, blackened interior. He found one of his daughters in a shed behind the ruin. He buried her. His wife and other daughter had been thrown back into the fire. He found some of their blackened bones and buried those.

The jawhawkers fought for the Union; Quantrill and his guerrillas fought against them. And the next time Quantrill was in the neighborhood, Smitty went to him. He rode straight as an arrow.

"You don't look like no kind of gunman I ever saw," Quantrill laughed. The most dangerous guerrilla leader in the South was what the tabloids called him. He was half drunk. He was always at least half drunk. Drunk or sober he was a dead shot and a murderer. Right now his eyes beheld Smitty with the curious gaze of the sated predator.

"No, sir. I done told you abut my family. I'd like to ride with you. I can cook your grub for you."

Well, Quantrill's eyes lit up. Half the kids in the countryside wanted to ride with him, but he was god-awful tired of hardtack and beans. "Take the oath," he said.

Smitty was hoping he could take lives in exchange for the lives that had been stolen from him, but he found out he couldn't. He carried the J.W. Dance pistol. He even fired it in a sort of general fashion. But he never wanted to cut down a man himself.

Others were not as particular. Some men carried five or six repeating pistols and were dead shots with them on horseback or afoot. They were more than a match for the average Union conscript fresh from the rat warrens of Detroit or New York or Chicago, each carrying a single-shot rifle he'd never fired before in his life.

In the four more years he had to live, Quantrill personally killed three or four hundred men. Bloody Bill Anderson, another guerrilla leader, kept a silk thong that he put a knot in for each one of his victims.

Most of the guerrillas were ordinary murderers. Some, like Smitty, were decent men who'd been caught up in a particularly savage region of a particularly savage war. Some were extraordinary murderers. Jesse James was like that. Slight, pretty as a girl, and just fifteen when Quantrill's men rode into Lawrence to sack it and kill "every male-thing" that lived in that town. Jesse was special. His big, soft-spoken brother, Frank, wasn't cut from the ordinary mold either.

Cole Younger had ready wit and a taste for practical jokes. A man could appeal to Cole Younger's sense of honor, and he had been known to turn a prisoner loose from time to time.

John Slocum. Slocum came to the guerrillas late, when the war was almost over. He was a veteran of the eastern campaigns. There were a few regulars in with Quantrill—men who'd fought with Bragg in Tennessee—but Slocum was the only one who'd actually followed Marse Robert and his splendid Army of Northern Virginia.

He never did share the guerrilla's blood lust. Oh, he'd fight, all right. He was as quick with his pistols as any of them. Maybe Cole Younger was a heartbeat faster, and maybe Quantrill was a mite better with a rifle at a thousand yards, but Slocum was as fast as an eyeblink and calmly dangerous.

They were all skinny. The last year of that war they were eating their own horses, but Slocum was the skinniest among them.

The guerrillas had cultivated certain habits of calculated ferocity. They came, they fought, they killed. They were routinely fearless. None of them expected to see the end of the war, and most of them didn't.

The guerrilla bands broke up under the steady pressure of the outraged Union army and civilian jayhawkers. All Quantrill's riders had prices on their heads.

The Yanks caught Bloody Bill. Fifty of them hiding in a blackberry thicket when Bloody Bill rode into range. The ambushers blew him out of the saddle and cut off his head and carried it home on a stake.

The James brothers ran for their home place. Maybe the law wouldn't come after them. Cole and James Younger rode off toward the Indian nations.

Quantrill headed for Kentucky. He had kin near Louisville.

One fine morning Smitty found himself with nothing to fight for and nobody to cook for, either. He was a man made for peace, and the war was over. Smitty scratched his head. He unhitched the two horses that had been used to draw his cook wagon/ammunition wagon/ambulance. He mounted one horse and tied the other on behind. Besides the two horses and the J.W. Dance wrapped in oil cloth inside his saddlebags, he took nothing out of the war except his life. And that fact filled him with wonderment.

Smitty went west across the wide Missouri, and there were plenty of other ex-Rebs who flowed west with him. Because he'd ridden with the guerrillas, he listened when the talk in the saloons turned to the war or famous badmen. Jesse and Frank were getting quite a reputation. Quantrill was shot to death by some Yankee officers. Cole Younger was thought to be robbing banks, and there were other Youngers who rode with him.

John Slocum was alive. He'd been seen in Texas, Montana, New Mexico, and California. He'd robbed a bank in Austin, held up a train in Dakota, scouted for Custer, rode with the Indians against Custer—hell, there were a million stories. From time to time Smitty heard a tale he halfway believed. He heard John Slocum lost every dime he owned in a poker game at

Adobe Wells and walked out the next morning across the desert with nothing but his rifle and sixgun.

Like the rest of them then, John Slocum was on the run. Riding the high trails through the backcountry, using the fords and the desert wells only the outlaws and the Indians know. He'd been seen on the Missouri, and he'd been seen at the forts. He'd taken up with a few women, but none of them was particularly notorious, and saloon talk rarely included their last names.

He was nearby, dangerous, alone. . . .

"Maybe he'll take on a job for us," Smitty said.

Murchison thought it over. There was no law in the territory a man didn't make himself. His few friends were cattlemen, and they sure weren't gonna help him round up his sheep.

Murchison clipped the tip off a Havana with his sharp teeth. He felt pretty damn good, and for the first time in weeks his fingers weren't cold. "It's worth a shot. You and Renfrew button up Muleshoe. I'll want the hay ready for the horses and every one of the animals rubbed down and grained. Tomorrow morning, soon as it's light to travel, we hit the road."

Mary Anne's hand jumped to her mouth. "Papa, you know what the doctor said."

He grinned. The fierceness of his grin reminded her of how he'd been before he got sick. "Honey," he said, "so long as they got our sheep up on that mountainside, they got my seeds in the vise. You'll pardon the language, because that's how it is. Either this Slocum will lend a hand or tell us to get packin'. Makes no nevermind. If we don't get the woolies home before the weather breaks, there won't be no Muleshoe. Nothin' but a couple sad old punchers hangin' out in the saloon tellin' each other how it used to be. Smitty never fought in his life, and he's carryin' iron now. So I figure I ain't got so much to lose no matter how the chips fall.''

Mary Anne Murchison set her chin in the air. "I'm going too," she said bravely.

"Of course you'll go," he snapped. "Who else will take my arm if you don't? Daughter, you can follow me right into the jaws of hell." He was short of breath when he finished specifying. Regretfully, he eyed the Havana he'd licked but not fired up. He stuck the unlit stogie in the corner of his mouth. "Me, you, and Smitty leave for Silver City."

"What about me?" Jack Renfrew asked.

"You ain't so much use as the rest of us," Murchison said.

Renfrew turned red and his hands knotted up.

"You stay behind and look after the horses," Murchison said. "If somebody wants to take those horses away from you, let 'em." He chuckled a mean chuckle. "I'd just plumb hate to see you get hurt protecting them."

3

At six thousand feet it was already winter. Gusts of snow blew against the glistening sides of the two Denver & Rio Grande locomotives, melted where they were blasted with heat from the fireboxes, and pattered on the windows of the only passenger car. Mary Anne Murchison stared out the window and wondered how any country could be uglier or more frightening than this.

The mining operations upstream had deposited thousands of tons of overburden and waste in the dark yellow of the creek's waters. At streamside, waste froze thick and yellow like butter. The trees were cut back for three hundred yards from the tracks. The forests of stumps looked like wooden legs dusted lightly with snow. Mary Anne shuddered.

Her father had been jovial this morning, ate a bigger breakfast than usual, and almost decided to leave the buckboard behind. He eyed his old saddle horse with real longing, but prudence prevailed—and a good thing, too. With every switchback the locomotive climbed, his color got worse.

Smitty rode silent. He had a pocket testament open in his lap. His lips moved as he traced the words, sentence by sentence, line by line. He still wore the

SILVER CITY SHOOTOUT 45

J.W. Dance in its Confederate holster, and Mary Anne's father carried a short-barreled banker's Colt in a vest holster. The butt tinkled his watch chain now and again. He breathed through his open mouth and his eyes bulged. He looked awfully uncomfortable—too uncomfortable to speak. Mary Anne held his hand because she couldn't think of anything else to do. She looked out the window because even the ugliness was better than her own father's straining face.

Except for them and the conductor, dozing across a pair of seats in the front, the coach was empty. It was nearly new. The seats were covered with blue velour, nappy and slick to the touch. The carpet runner in the aisle was new too. The shades on the coach were uniform: half up, half down, and the same beige color. There wasn't a single bullet hole in any of the windows, and the gold leaf of the window trim sparkled.

It took two 2-4-2 Baldwin locomotives back to back to push one passenger car and the boxcar up the terrible grade to Silver City. Sometimes the track clung to the sides of awful precipices; sometimes it disappeared into tunnels bored through rock. Building this twenty-mile spur had taken lives. "A Chinaman a mile" was how the local wags put it.

Silver City was to be the largest, busiest mining town on the North American continent. Its brochures claimed:

TREASURE HOUSE GRANDER THAN
VIRGINIA CITY, NEVADA
THIRTY TONS OF FINE SILVER PER DAY

PLACER GOLD IN NEARBY STREAMS
OREGON AND SHORT LINE RAILROAD
ACCOMMODATIONS FOR SPECULATORS AND TOURISTS

After a long tunnel the little train burst into the sunlight again. For a moment it seemed like the engineer had decided to imitate bird travel, as though the coach hung on nothing more substantial than air. The trestle stuck to the sheer rock rushing by, and on the left there was nothing but air. Miles of air.

Mary Anne wished the shades drawn but said nothing. She went into her reticule and took out knitting. She was a terrible handworker with poor coordination and less interest. The scarf she was knitting was a project many years old and unlikely to be finished. Her fingers got busy making one clumsy stitch after another. The car wheels screamed and squealed as the train lurched against the curves. Mary Anne clamped her lips together.

They passed above the timberline onto a wide plain dotted with full-grown trees that wouldn't come up to a man's waist. They passed a miner's shanty. Another one. A couple of buckboards abandoned in the brush, and the ax scars where someone had cut away pieces for firewood. The snow swooped and gusted, and a locomotive hooted its plaintive call.

The conductor yawned and stretched. He scratched his belly through a convenient gap in his blue coat. "You best keep a sharp eye on that snow," he said. "We've got one more scheduled run up here. If the snow's deep on the tracks, I expect we'll just give it up as a bad job."

The train hooted past rusty sidetracks serving one mine or another, the tracks dark brown with rust. The mine buildings that appeared out of the snow were gray unpainted ramshackle things with the loneliness of all the machines man makes and abandons.

"Keep a sharp eye on the weather," the conductor repeated. "Or you'll be wintering right here in Silver City." The train hooted happily at an abandoned crossing. Gray houses, gray picket fences, the occasional bright spot of color—a blue shed, a bright green set of shutters—but mostly gray, white, pale brown.

The conductor returned to his seat. He didn't look out the windows. He'd seen Silver City before.

The depot was quite new, freshly painted, and had shiny padlocks on the waiting room and the baggage room, too. They dropped the boxcar ramp and unloaded their buckboard right there on the station platform. Not that anyone was there to object.

Smitty and the conductor got J.D. loaded and wrapped in an enormous rug. He didn't say one word, and his breathing was more like gasping than breathing. Already the conductor was swinging his bull's-eye lantern and the locomotives were building a head of steam.

No return customers. No baggage. No passengers. No freight.

Five-twenty P.M. Already the light was going dim, like somebody pulling a rug out from under your feet. The depot stood somewhat above the town, and rows of buildings lay below them, glistening in the last wash of light.

Only two months ago Silver City had been a town of thirty thousand souls. That was before the silver price fell and it got so it was more money to get the silver out of the ground than to leave it there. The miners pulled out of Silver City. And when the miners went, the bartenders and liverymen and dancing girls and assayers and grocers and market hunters and coopers and carpenters and millwrights and preachers left too.

The wind walked the narrow streets of Silver City like an honored guest. The coyotes howled a stone's throw from the Methodist church, and tumbleweeds bounced and banked up against the Silver City Bank ("Assets, $39,000").

Silver City had been laid out like a Greek cross with one Main Street and a couple of spurs. The town pointed toward the creek where placer miners had first found the heavy silver ore.

Smitty had the reins. His holster was unbuttoned, and Mary Anne wondered that she hadn't noticed him doing that. One hand on the reins and one beside his open holster.

The spare saddle horse trotted behind. It had seemed cold to Mary Anne back at Muleshoe, but this was more winter and chilled her to the bone.

The *clop clop* of the horse's hooves. Released from their long confinement in the boxcar, they wanted to stretch out, but Smitty's hands on the reins held them in.

Blank black windows. Drawn curtains or shades.

A stagecoach with one broken wheel and the rear door open and swinging in the wind. The stagecoach carried a couple of solid leather trunks on top; the trunks looked as good as new.

The windows were shattered in the mercantile, and broken glass lay across the boardwalk, catching the last of the faint blue light.

"Is that a lantern?" Mary Anne was pointing up a side street where a glimmer shone.

"Sure enough," Smitty said. And Mary Anne was glad to hear the relief in his voice. She didn't want her fear to be unique.

The yellow gleam of a kerosene lantern peeped through the windows of a long, two-story building. THE GRIZZLY BEAR SALOON.

"I could wet my whistle," Smitty said.

Old J.D. didn't say a word. His breathing was stentorian and harsh. The snow was melting where it touched the horse's backs but sticking on the saddlebags and harnesses. A tumbleweed bounced past them, taking great five-foot hops, light and dry as a feather.

Mary Anne shivered. There was a red checked curtain over the saloon window. The light poured out of the gap above the curtain like a warm wall. Music played. Inside, someone was playing a tinny piano. The tune was "Dixie." The pianist concluded with a great crash of keys, and the silence was very loud.

"Miss, if you'll take your father's arm, we can help him inside."

Murchison's mouth gapped open. "Inside," he agreed.

The piano began again. The tune was "Dixie" again.

Murchison carried enough weight on his own legs for Smitty to fumble the door open.

"Hello," Smitty shouted. "Damn! It's winter out here, sure enough!"

The piano tinkled on its merry way, the keys depressing and rising back into place. It was a player piano, and behind the glass you could see the cylindrical roll turning the little steel nubs that made the music, glittering as it turned.

The Grizzly Bear Saloon was a high-class place. The walls held a couple of buffalo heads and a large silvertip head in the place of honor. Underneath the trophies was a huge rock fireplace, big enough to roast an ox. A tall cylindrical wood stove was piped into the fireplace, and the iron sides glowed cheerfully.

Chairs were up on the tables. All but one chair and one table.

Mary Anne Murchison could hear the slaps as the man in the black suit set down his cards.

He looked up. "There's whiskey behind the bar," he said. "Help yourself." *Slap slap* of the cards and the piano tinkling out its Confederate tune.

Smitty got Murchison seated next to that stove with his legs on another seat and the rug up to his shoulders.

The bar was ornately carved, with leaded-glass cabinets and four sets of beer handles, one per bartender on a busy Saturday night. Smitty found a bottle that claimed to be brandy and pulled out the cork. He held the glass up to old J.D.'s lips himself, and the sick man swallowed and choked and swallowed again.

Mary Anne marched to the back of the saloon. She had her hands on her hips. "Look here," she said. "Do you own this place?"

His hair was as black as the underside of a raven's wing where the sun can't fade it. His eyebrows were that same dark color. His face was calm, thoughtful, and pale—the gambler's pale. His suit was top quality, and closer up she could see the stripes in the dark fabric. His shirt was brilliant white, tied with a floppy yellow foulard. The foulard was the only bit of color about him. His hands were extremely long, almost misshapen. His hat, a black Stetson, lay on the table beside the cards.

A bottle of champagne was open in an ice bucket, and the glass at his elbow was half full of golden wine.

He examined her long and calm. He smiled so briefly that a moment later she wasn't sure he had smiled. "Yes, ma'am," he said. "I'm the proprietor."

Mary Anne Murchison asked if there were rooms upstairs to let, as her father was quite ill and needed a bed.

Again that too flashing smile. "Ten rooms and a suite at the south end of the hall. Take what suits you."

"Sir, my father is a considerable burden."

He nodded. He stacked his cards neatly in the middle of the green baize.

"Bad ticker," Smitty explained. Murchison's eyes were closed now; his breathing was easier.

The black-clad man stopped dead. His strange green eyes gleamed like a cat's eyes at night. His right hand hooked his frock coat aside. When his hand came to rest, the fingertips were very close to a Colt gun butt. "I know you from somewhere," he said.

"Yes, sir." Smitty nodded his head very vigorously. He removed his hat to facilitate identification. "'Spect you do. We rode together during the war. Smitty. I was Quantrill's belly robber."

This time the smile lasted longer. "My apologies, Smitty. I wasn't expecting to see you."

"You're John Slocum?" Mary Anne demanded.

"The same."

"Mary Anne Murchison. This is my father, J.D. Murchison, of the Muleshoe."

Slocum nodded. He'd heard of Muleshoe.

With girlish charm Mary Anne asked, "Where is everybody, anyway?"

"Who ain't hither is yon," Slocum said. He eyed the ailing rancher with some displeasure. If the man was to die here, it'd be the devil planting him. The ground was froze a foot down.

The stove cracked and popped, and Smitty warmed his hands. "Mighty spooky kind of place," he ventured. "A real ghost town."

Slocum dropped a nickle into the piano's mechanism and it tinkled itself back to life. "Seems like a long time since the war," Smitty said, raising his voice over the music.

"Seems like yesterday," John Slocum said. "I don't suppose I can interest you in a friendly game."

Smitty said, "If you got any grub, I'd be pleased to cook up some dinner for all of us. We never brought any provisions because we didn't expect . . . this."

"Silver City? Oh, you'll get used to it. It's nice and quiet. Things fall down. The rats and the cats fought it out in Murphy's empty granary, and that was the most excitement there's been all week.''

"Do you mean to winter here?" Mary Anne asked.

"Why not?"

"Well, I'd get awfully lonesome." Mary Anne made a cute face.

Something flickered behind his eyes. "Lonesome ain't the worst thing there is," he said.

Smitty turned to admire the neat details of the saloon. "I'll bet it was really something when the town was booming."

"It was quite a show," John Slocum smiled. "We'd get a pretty rowdy crowd here on a Saturday night."

J.D. Murchison croaked, "Damn, it's hell bein' alive."

"Maybe so," Smitty retorted. "But you are a whole lot better lookin' than you was."

"I seen healthier lookin' dead," Slocum noted.

J.D. Murchison was strong enough to be helped up the stairs. Slocum insisted they take the suite. "The single rooms are just cribs," he said.

Mary Anne Murchison blushed scarlet. Behind these skimpy little doors the girls had taken their customers. Though she knew it was a silly fear, she expected a door to open and a painted face to leer at her.

The suite was surprisingly comfortable. Adjoining rooms with one double bed and a daybed. The room was quite clean but slightly dusty. The bed was covered with a nubby white counterpane.

"I can take care of him now," she said when they had her father propped up with pillows on the comfortable bed.

From somewhere inside his sickness Murchison managed a frown. "Slocum," he said.

"Yeah?"

"Job of work . . ."

He wanted to say more but wasn't able. Slocum told Smitty he'd find a couple of elk hindquarters hung in the pantry. Slocum followed the cook downstairs.

When Mary Anne was satisfied with her father's comfort, she adjusted her makeup in the big dresser mirror. They'd been traveling thirteen hours, and she wasn't untouched, but she was undamaged.

The dark-haired proprietor was back at the baize table sipping champagne and laying out his solitaire hand. She sat beside him.

"You play cribbage? Gin? Honeymoon bridge? Poker?"

"I'm sorry. I don't play cards."

"I'm sorrier. I don't get much chance for a game."

"How long's it been . . . like this?"

"Passengers got on the train three weeks ago Wednesday. I know they was the last. I saw them off. When they was almost out of sight, I tipped my hat."

"You were glad they were gone?"

He lifted his eyes then and really looked at her. His eyes tapped her wide blue ones and queried their innocence. The woman didn't understand how sometimes a man could sicken of himself, his work, and the whole damn human species. He diverted her. "What brings you to Silver City?"

"You, John Slocum."

The cards came from his hands in perfect order. "You my enemy? Kin to somebody I killed?" His face was blank, his eyes were very alive.

"No." She was surprised enough to be rude. "Have you killed many men, Mr. Slocum?"

"Several." He folded the long string of cards and turned it over. He poured himself another glass of champagne but didn't offer her any.

"Mr. Slocum," she said, "we need your help. We'll pay you good."

Smitty stuck his head back into the big room but withdrew when he saw the pair in conversation.

He grinned at her. "It'd be hard to find much to buy in Silver City," he said. It was the first time he'd smiled. It made him look very much younger. She'd been thinking he was in his middle thirties, but he couldn't be much more than twenty-five.

"I suppose the biggest saloon owner in Silver City would hardly lack for anything."

He rested his long hands beside the deck. "There are a few things I lack," he said.

Coyly, "Oh, I thought a man like you—you'd have everything: whiskey, cards, shelter against the weather." The wind picked up outside and shook the windows in their frames. The tiny hard granules of snow rattled against the glass.

"Yep," he admitted. " 'Course it's hard to kill anybody if there ain't anybody near, and whenever I feel the strong urge to take human life, I have to remind myself that one day the silver price'll come up and I can set to killin' and maimin' my neighbors again." He rolled a quirly and moistened the paper.

He popped the tip of a lucifer with his thumbnail and it burst into fire.

"Ma'am," he said, "I learned a few things during the war. War needs men willing to take up guns and shoot them at whoever the generals point out. I was no different. General says, 'John Slocum, you just stand up on that parapet and pop you a bluebelly officer,' I did that. And if someone else told me to take a detachment of sharpshooters up on Little Round Top, I did that, too. And if someone said I should ride with Quantrill, well, that was the same as all the other orders I took during the war. Now maybe I learn slow, but I learned there's times I never want to work for the other man. One of those times is when I have a gun in my hand. I don't know what sort of trouble you have, but I'm sorry for it. You're a handsome woman. You ought to have no trouble getting men to kill for you."

She reached and took a sip from his glass of champagne. It was awfully good. Good as the stuff she'd tasted back east. "You," she said. The single word hung in the air like a hot-air balloon twisting and twirling in the sunlight. Slocum's neck hair stood up on the back of his neck for no reason he could name.

She sipped the golden liquid. She moistened her lips. Her eyes were blue-willow plates. Her breasts heaved against the practical, high-collared gray traveling suit. A wisp of hair had escaped from under her hat. It was as yellow as new-minted gold coins.

"Now that you mention it," Slocum drawled, "there is one thing I lack."

She smiled at him, and her lips were ripe fruit.

He tapped his finger on the green baize table—tap, tap, tap. "I don't suppose you'd like to tell me about it," he began slowly.

"Smitty knows more about it than I do. He was there."

They didn't say very much more until Smitty brought plates from the saloon's well-equipped kitchen. They waited. They looked at each other. From time to time she blushed.

"Eat it while it's hot," Smitty intoned.

The elk steaks were pounded and breaded in some kind of flour before they were fried up. The crust fell away with the touch of a fork, and the meat inside was steaming and pink. Home-fried potatoes, canned tomatoes, canned beans, and biscuits. It was a real good meal, and once Mary Anne got to eating she was hungrier than she thought she'd been.

Smitty sat with them. He had a smaller plate than the others. Smitty liked to cook but he never liked to eat.

Slocum said, "There's one tap under pressure. Anybody want a schooner of beer with their grub?"

The ate slowly, steadily, with no talking to interrupt the serious business of fueling the fires. Smitty went back to the kitchen for seconds, though his own second helping was minute. Slocum lit a Havana. He offered Mary Anne one, and she was flattered. A few European women smoked in the privacy of their own rooms, but only actresses and women of loose (or artistic) morals smoked in the States.

Once his pipe was drawing good, Smitty asked, "What do you think about sheep?"

"No opinion," Slocum replied.

"You feel any particular animosity?" Smitty was slipping up on his subject. The last time he'd seen John Slocum was in the heat of battle, and both Slocum's Colts had been taking lives, and Smitty treated him as if he might be touchy. Right touchy.

"No sheep critter ever did any harm to me or mine," Slocum said. "You got a sheep war at Muleshoe?"

Smitty told him. How Teton Jackson and his boys wouldn't let the riders take the sheep down to winter quarters.

"They killed a boy, you say?" Slocum asked.

"Gave him no chance at all," Smitty said.

"I have heard of sheepherders gettin' burned out and I've heard of night riders chasin' the sheep over a buffalo jump and I heard of hoorawin' in town and a few broken bones and plenty hard feelings, but this is the first I ever heard of somebody gettin' killed over it."

"Do you know Teton Jackson?"

A grimace. "Can't say I ever had that pleasure."

"Red Smart? Con Hennessey? That hombre they call Butch?"

"Smart was in Denver when I was. He wasn't anything to fear coming right on at you, but once you crossed him, you'd have to keep an eye in the back of your head at night. Natural-born backshooter that one."

She breathed. "Muleshoe needs you. Without your help, we'll never get those animals off the mountainside. They'll starve, John."

"Uh-huh. Smitty, why don't you go put a couple

more logs on that fire? That stove just naturally eats timber.''

His eyes got very distant and he tapped his finger again. It didn't matter whether Mary Anne was there or not. His eyes were seeing old battles.

After the war, John Slocum had made one good attempt to settle down. On his own land, a chunk of ground called Slocum's Stand that had been in Slocum hands since Lord Fairfax got that enormous land grant direct from the king. They weren't rich or fancy folks—just hardworking farmers, healthy and tough. Slocums fought in the Revolution, in Andy Jackson's war of 1812, and Slocum's father had ridden with Zack Taylor, storming the walls of Monterrey, in far-off Mexico.

Slocum males had fought America's wars as plain soldiers, and they took to fighting like it was natural to them. John Slocum enlisted as a private and made captain before the end. John Slocum's brother died in Pickett's doomed charge at Gettysburg. After the war, John Slocum returned to his family's land. The land was coveted by a carpetbagger and Slocum shot him down. It was a fair fight—but the carpetbagger was a Yankee judge and Slocum left just ahead of the law. Since then he'd been a gold prospector, trail boss, gambler, and he'd ridden shotgun for more than his fair share of dangerous loads. He'd won the Grizzly Bear Saloon in a four-day marathon poker game. It was a good business for exactly six weeks before the silver market crashed. Slocum had enjoyed working the business side of the saloon. Slocum's houseman took a dime rake-off from every pot and supplied the cards—all honest decks. The booze was good, the girls were amiable, and nobody had to worry about getting knocked on the head or cheated. The Grizzly Bear Saloon did a land-office business for six short weeks.

John Slocum hadn't quite made up his mind what he wanted to do next. Since he didn't know, he waited. He felt no particular pressure to make a decision. Wasn't his life his own?

"There's one more train out of Silver City," Smitty said. "If it don't snow too bad they'll make one more run tomorrow. Me and the Murchisons have to be on it."

"Uh-huh."

She put her hand on his arm. "Please, Mr. Slocum. My father says we can pay you a percentage of the sheep you bring down."

"Ma'am," he drawled lazily, "you are talking to a property owner. The first citizen of Silver City. What could you offer better than that?"

She licked her lips. Smitty looked away. After a moment he started taking dishes back to the kitchen. When he had them all, he kicked the door shut with the back of his heel. For a while they could hear him crashing around in there.

"That was a fine meal," she said.

"Uh-huh."

"Mr. Slocum? What do you mean to do now?"

He hauled his gold hunter out of his vest and checked the time. "I mean to put some more wood on that fire, damp it down, and go upstairs. Mr. Whitman. I read his book before I go to bed."

She swallowed. Her mouth seemed full of glue. "And me?"

He grinned at her, short and sweet.

While he fussed with the stove, she looked in on her father. When she pushed the door open, she was half prepared to find him . . . gone. But, a miracle: His color was good, and his breathing was easier. She bent and gave him a dutiful-daughter peck on his forehead. That's how she thought of herself: the dutiful daughter. She heard Slocum's boots coming upstairs. He hesitated, then went down the hall where the other big suite was located.

Mary Anne Murchison stepped behind a screen to remove her whalebone corset and three of her four camisoles. Her body felt fine: tingly. A tiny dab of perfume went behind her ears. With a funny smile she dabbed the perfume on the tops of her breasts.

She was no virgin. She'd had two rather unsatisfactory love affairs. One, a young man from Princeton who was studying for the ministry; the other, a brief fling with an Italian count—three days of rather strained decadence. Her chaperone had been ill with the fever, and once that worthy lady recovered, the affair ended—to the relief (undisguised) of both lovers.

When she first set eyes on John Slocum, she thought: How interesting! Nothing so far had changed her opinion. Now she was delighted because she was combining inclination with what she took to be her duty.

The lights were low on the saloon floor. Old Smitty was still banging around in the kitchen.

She tiptoed down the end of the hall. Just a crack of light under the door. She hesitated and then came in without knocking. Slocum was sitting on a purple velvet couch. He was bootless and wore no shirt. Mary Anne Murchison repressed a gasp. His chest was broad and nearly hairless, his belly hard. A wedgelike scar in his side must have been a knife (bayonet?) wound, and those puckered marks on his right arm and shoulder surely came from bullets.

He looked like an old cowhide, scratched and ripped by a hundred random collisions. He closed his book and set it down. So she wouldn't have to look at his wounds, she picked it up and read out loud at random:

"In the close of the day with its light and the fields of spring, and the farmers preparing their crops,
In the large unconscious scenery of my land with its lakes and forests . . ."

She cocked her head. She said, "Are you a reader, then, Mr. Slocum?"

"I've passed many an hour with Mr. Whitman for company."

He took the book from her hand. He looked at her until she blushed and said, "Look at all the terrible scars you have." Her hand went out (of its own accord) to touch the puckered flesh in the meat of his shoulder. The scar was tough flesh. The skin was quite soft. "You must have had an adventurous life."

"No, ma'am," he said sincerely. "It was just

plumb bad luck. Some men go on through life and ain't no bullet molded that can find them. Others get struck regularly, and I suppose I'm one of those.'' His hand traced the downy hair on the back of her hand. Her hand was safe touching his surprisingly soft skin. He had a mole to the side of one nipple, dark, no bigger than a match head. She touched that mole as if it were a conduit to his heart. He covered her hand with his.

After a bit he stood. Her dress opened. He undid each hook and eye so it hung open like a robe. He kissed her. His hands slid inside, above her white silk camisole, around to her bare shoulders. His hands were very warm. His mouth and hers breathed into each other. She was pressed into his strong thighs, and his excitement touched hers and she gasped.

She hadn't known it could be this way. It had never been like this before.

He took her dress off her arms and everything seemed slow to her, awfully slow, like she was underwater or in the languorous world between dreaming and sleep.

He touched the globes of her breasts like he had never seen a woman's breasts before—like her breasts were wonderful.

''Come,'' he said.

He lowered the wick in the kerosene lamp so it shed its low golden glow over the white sheets and the white pillows of the bed.

It looked like an arena, an altar, a table of plenty. The whiteness of the sheets was opalescent in the light. Her breasts were dusky, and her long golden hair darkened and lightened, like a flowing river of gold.

Her breasts were full and young. The nipples were very tiny but angled upward in excitement.

Her camisole lay on the floor behind her. He stepped out of his pants.

"Oh my," she said. She wondered if she was going to be hurt. It didn't seem awful to be hurt by his cock. She burned so much. "Oh my."

When they lay down on those white sheets she held him away for a long moment. She looked into his eyes and she found gentleness and laughter in the back of his green green eyes. She could feel the head of his erection against her knee. Then, delicate as a swan, she stretched out to touch his lips.

She found the heat of his mouth and she melted under his touch as he gave her back to her own flesh, as he touched her into herself, as he caressed her as she had never been touched before. Never before. Her legs flopped open and closed and flopped open again. She said something that came out a moan.

She felt the pressure of his hips against the inside of her splayed thighs. She was pinned by his weight. As he came into her, the air left her lungs in a cry, parting all before him, extinguishing her pain.

She jumped to meet him, to make them one.

They began the dance—the teasing touching of the dance. She distanced herself and he called her back. He went away and she called his name. Their sweat commingled on her belly, and skin slapped against skin as the bedsprings hummed and twanged.

Because she trusted him, she gave her love like rain.

They lay silent on the sheets breathing hard, hand in hand. Both stared at the pressed squares of the tin ceiling and thought their own thoughts.

They joined again when they were rested, and drank the rest of the champagne before Slocum blew out the light. In the darkness, Mary Anne Murchison did several things she never thought she'd do on Slocum's body, and he returned the favor.

4

They slept for a few hours, between four and seven. Next morning they didn't say anything to each other. They'd done all the talking they could.

J.D. Murchison felt better. His weakened heart had managed the altitude change. He hollered until Slocum came into the room, and the two men talked for several hours, setting the terms.

John Slocum was to have a percentage of the sheep he saved.

"The percentage starts at five thousand animals," Murchison said. "Anything less than that, you don't get a dime."

Hell, Slocum didn't care.

Smitty made a big lunch for all of them. He took every scrap of meat out of the storehouse and set it outside for the scavengers.

The snow was blowing but wasn't covering anything. The train would make one more trip out of Silver City.

John Slocum put his neat black gladstone in the back of the Murchison buckboard. He looked at the Grizzly Bear Saloon for a long time. The wind kicked up snow devils down the street. Carefully, he locked the front door and gave it a shake.

Smitty looked his question.

"I never owned a saloon before," Slocum said. He tossed the key into the street. It twinkled and disappeared.

J.D. Murchison's health improved every switchback they dropped, and several thousand feet lower, in the foothills, he was almost his old self. Longingly, he looked at Slocum's cigar. "Damn it, boy," he said. "I ain't supposed to have any of those, but you'd do me a service if you was to blow some of that smoke in my direction."

Smitty was in the front of the car consulting timetables with the conductor. They'd have to change trains at Montpelier.

The engineer and fireman were cranking their locomotive pretty hard. The locomotive hooted. The engineer had a ready hand on his whistle and bell cord since leaving Silver City. The train crew was glad this was their last trip up to the deserted silver town.

Mary Anne was commenting on the scenery, which was rather beautiful in a slightly grotesque but spectacular fashion. She cooed and identified scenic vistas. Her voice lilted and sung.

"Well, ain't she chipper," her father commented with a glance at the tall black-clad stranger sitting beside him.

"Seems so," Slocum replied shortly.

"Wonder what could have made her so. She's generally a solemn girl."

"Uh-huh."

"Tell me about yourself, Slocum."

"What do you want to know, Murchison?"

"Well I was kind of wondering who you are, you know. I don't have the time most men have to pursue a leisurely acquaintanceship."

"I fought for the South. I never married. I got no living kin."

"Well, that isn't very much to say."

"Nope. Sometimes it seemed that way to me, too. Who's Teton Jackson?"

"Local badhat. He came west to be a mountain man, or so I'm told. Spent a couple seasons trapping for beaver before he began to follow his natural inclination to steal other men's cows."

"Why's he after your sheep?"

"It's the trail. He runs cows over that rail, and he don't want anybody pasturing up there or using that trail but him. Somebody actually sees him with a herd of stolen critters and sooner or later that identification could get him hung. 'Least that's how I got it figured."

"Uh-huh."

"Smitty said you rode with Quantrill."

Slocum leaned back in the seat and looked out the window.

"I heard you was pals of Cole Younger and the James brothers."

John Slocum watched the trees go by. Down here they were standard-size again and he liked them that way. He drew on his Havana and tipped his hat down over his eyes, like a man planning a snooze.

"Damn it. Most men answer me when I speak!"

From under his slanted hat, Slocum replied, "Man gets old, gets to fixing to die, and that naturally makes him a little rough. Like an old mossyback, been captain of the herd so long he forgets he's just meat

on the hoof like everybody. I don't answer your
questions because its none of your affair who I've
been and what I've done. I don't take it as mannerly
for you to ask, and a younger man would pay some
cost for bothering me that way. If you want a Havana, Mr. Murchison, just light it yourself. You ain't
got so long to live you can't enjoy a smoke."

Murchison was angry halfway through the speech,
but before Slocum finished he was laughing. As
suggested, he plucked a cigar from the younger man's
breast pocket, and with relish he lit up and took a
puff.

He replied to his daughter's distress with a sunny
grin. He waved his cigar. "What the hell," he said.
"What the hell."

The train pulled into Montpelier about eight that
night. The southbound left in the morning. It was a
white-painted town with green trim, rather more uniform than customary on the frontier, as though it had
been occupied by sober, industrious men for fifty
years or more. The streets were broad and pleasant
and lined with saplings that promised to be shade
trees one day. This was a Mormon community, and
there weren't so many women on the streets. Polyg-
amy was a real problem for the Saints, not something
they advertised.

Montpelier had its Drover's Arms, a small clean
hotel that didn't serve alcohol in its unpretentious,
spotless dining room. Smitty thought the food was
underspiced and overcooked, and allowed as how he
could do better and often had. Slocum ate heartily,
undisturbed by the absence of whiskey and wine.

Afterward, he asked the waitress for a toothpick and the location of the nearest poker game.

"Oh," she said, shocked, "we don't hold with gambling in Montpelier. Montpelier is a family town."

Fine. Slocum retired early with his copy of Mr. Whitman's book. He halfway expected Mary Anne to tiptoe on down the hall to his room, but the hotel got quiet about ten and stayed that way. Apparently there was another little vice that didn't go on in Montpelier. That, or Mary Anne had bought and paid for him last night. Not a good thought to go to sleep on. He turned out the light.

John Slocum dreamed of his family farm back in Georgia, in the wintertime when it was brushed with snow and Chilly Draft froze over and he and his brother would go down to the pond and slide and laugh and fall down. The dream was so vivid he awoke in the dark and didn't know where he was. By his lucifer it was just three in the morning. Montpelier at night was as quiet as Silver City. Quieter maybe, without the coyotes howling. He wondered what he was doing in this town, why he was working for the Murchisons. In the dark, lying with his hands under his head, it didn't seem like a job that'd lead anywhere. It seemed like another chance to get his head blown clean off. Well, maybe that's what he wanted. If he really wanted what he was supposed to—a wife, a family, a home—he supposed he'd have it by now. There was a knack to that kind of work, and he didn't honestly think he had the knack. Day in, day out, plowing the same ground, facing the same woman across the breakfast table, calm with the kids, steady with neighbors and friends. Hell!

That was a job of work! Better take his chances getting his head blown off.

When he woke again just after six, he felt awful and wished he'd stayed in Silver City.

The hotel grub was better at breakfast, though Smitty growled that "nobody can ruin ham and grits and eggs," and he did have a point.

J.D. Murchison paid for all the rooms. It made John Slocum feel strange, having the other man pay for his accommodations.

The southbound pulled two boxcars, a mail car, a coach, and a parlor car at the rear of the train. The coach was full, so they paid the extra four bits to sit in the plush upholstered chairs of the parlor car. Slocum had a brandy. Murchison said, "You can bring me one of those too."

The train passed into Nevada Territory, rolling steadily southward. The stops were infrequent. Generally, Slocum got out to stretch his legs at the wood and water stops. Forewarned by the Drover's Hotel, they carried box lunches. "Not enough chicken," Smitty grumbled, "but their slaw is all right."

The country leveled. The seasons retreated. Rolling hills gave way to flat dry land dotted with mesas and buttes.

Once they scared up a small band of antelope and the passengers went to the windows to watch. One drummer stepped onto the observation platform, drew his pepperbox, and pulled the trigger. A cloud of black smoke and the drummer's arm jerked sharply upward by the recoil. The pronghorns galloped off unharmed. The drummer came back shaking his head. "I thought I had me one of those, for sure."

"Damn fool," Slocum said, just loud enough for the drummer to hear and force the red into the tips of his ears.

The depot at Seguro was ten miles west of town. The railroad hadn't thought it worth a bend in their tracks to get in closer.

No cabby at the tiny depot, and the stationmaster helped them unload their horses and buckboard.

The vacuum of the train's departure set the little station sign to swinging: SEGURO EL: 832.

"I hope we can find the herder you're looking for," Murchison said.

So did Slocum.

The town itself lay in the lee of the cliffs, and the road to it was as straight as an arrow. Seguro had twenty or so buildings and half those were sheds, horse barns, or stables. The largest building was a thirty-by-seventy windowless warehouse—the Seguro Wool Cooperative. Slocum supposed that was where they stored the stuff. Smells of evening meals cooked in the smallish adobe houses they passed. Kids outdoors playing in the dust stopped their play to gawk at the first strangers they'd seen in weeks.

The heart of Seguro was a Spanish-style plaza with the church facing the mercantile, catty-corner to the Seguro Grower's National Bank, which faced a low adobe structure that Slocum headed for right away, the others close behind.

The cantina was a single long room the proportions of a shoe box. The walls were covered with adobe except where bullets had chewed great chunks out of the hardened mud to expose the raw rock.

The cantina was jammed, and Murchison had to

think before he remembered this was Saturday night and all the riders for miles around were in town tonight to get drunk, get laid, and get into trouble. The design of the place wasn't so different from the Grizzly Bear Saloon. Like Slocum's joint, this one had a second story with a balcony. Girls hung over that balcony, four of them, dressed in simple flowery shifts. They wore bright glass jewelry and their hair was bound in ribbons. Two were Spanish, one clearly Indian, and one a thin-shanked, blond, tuberculer white. They called when John Slocum led his party into the room. They waved.

"Come on up here, amigo. We know how to treat you right."

"Leave the *rubia*. She can't do for you what I can do," one of the Spanish girls announced, pressing one finger to her more than ample bosom.

Slocum doffed his Stetson and proffered a deep bow, which was only very slightly mocking.

Men were bellied up to the bar three deep. The rickety tables were much less popular, and only a couple were occupied: three Mexicans talking with their heads very close together, and an Indian, dozing with his feet propped up on the chair facing him.

Conscious of the eyes on him, Murchison pulled out his daughter's chair and sat her down. He folded his hands. After thirty years in the West, he was good at waiting.

Unlike the Grizzly Bear Saloon, the cantina had no piano, player or otherwise. Slocum waited until men parted to let him get to the bar.

Some men spoke Spanish, some spoke in English, and some in what sounded like an Indian dialect—

Zuni, or maybe Navaho. Several dark-faced men spoke an unfamiliar language with whistles and queer sounds for words—rapid and singsong and strange.

The place was in a pretty good mood, it being pretty early in the evening, but later on hell was going to pop. Everybody was holding back until they had a few more drinks under their belts before they moved on to the next phase of the evening's entertainment.

"What you drinking?" Slocum had no room at the bar for his shoulders, and he screwed his head around to ask Smitty's order.

"Whatever you're havin'." Smitty wasn't a drinking man, never had been.

When Slocum had a bottle and glasses, he crooked his elbows into the bar and let his eyes drift casually over the crowd. The whiskey was trade whiskey: grain alcohol flavored with red pepper, molasses, a pinch of black gunpowder, and a chaw of tobacco for good luck. If you were lucky, it didn't make you blind. It always made you drunk.

John Slocum would never forget the time he rode into a Blackfoot encampment the day after whiskey traders had visited. The braves were crawling around looking for the furs the trappers had taken, and for their young women—because there was always a market for comely Blackfoot slaves. Most of the braves couldn't see, and several of them were already dead, and more would die before sunset. It was a godawful sight. . . . Slocum drained his glass of whiskey and felt it hit the pit of his stomach like a mortar shell. He belched fire. His eyes watered.

A couple of hawk-faced men were arguing. One

man topped the rising inflections of the other with
rising inflections of his own.

When the two of them stepped away from the bar,
Smitty saw that one of the two was a mannish tall
gaunt woman. Challenges went back and forth between them in that strange language. Smitty understood: somebody was asking somebody to put their
money where their mouth was. Both wore wide-
brimmed black sombreros. The man had a silver-coin
hatband and the woman wore strands of silver and
gold coins as necklaces. They both had trousers bloused
into their boots and wide sashes around their middles.

Both were young, dark-featured with the kind of
tan that comes from days and days under the merci-
less sun.

Now that the wager was set, the two acted happier,
joking with each other as they moved to the center of
the room. Plenty of men had joined the pair, laughing and making bets.

Another hawk-faced man hurriedly pulled tables
and chairs aside to form a narrow avenue between
them and a round slab of pin oak mounted on the
wall. The slab looked like a crude dart board decorated with the blue bull's-eye, a green circle surround-
ing that, and the red outside ring. The bull was about
the size of a man's heart.

The man spat into his hands and rubbed them on
the sides of his trousers. He was tall and quite graceful. He relaxed and carefully adjusted his scarf and
the cant of his hat.

His hand blurred. Afterward, Smitty said it was
"just like an ax splitting kindling on its way down

with all your steam behind it. That's what Arnaud
looked like.''

Two motions: His hand blurred to his waist; his
hand rose in a smooth arc, like the arc of someone
tossing a coin to a begger.

Thunk!

The pin-oak board shook against the adobe wall
and a stream of dust issued from underneath. The
brass hilt of the knife quivered, bright as a fishing
lure, near dead center in that board.

"Jesu!"

And now the man was bowing to the crowd and
laughing, and his white teeth were flashing as he told
his friends of the speed and accuracy of his knife, as
though they couldn't see for themselves. Men clapped
him on the back. He spilled a glass of whiskey down
his chin and wiped it on the back of his hand.

It was accidental when the crowd parted between
him and John Slocum and all at once the two men
were face to face.

"Ah, señor. You enjoy the speed of my knife?"

"It's quick."

"Very quick."

"If you say so." Slocum shrugged.

Arnaud's face went red under the dark tan. And
maybe he would have pressed the issue then and
there, but the crowd whistled and stomped their feet
and the tall woman called out, "Arnaud! How can
you have won the wager when I have not yet tried?"
And, laughing at him, she spat into the palms of her
hands and rubbed them on her trousers.

The crowd loved it.

She called out to one bartender for a beer mug,

and one hand passed it to another until she held the glass in her own hand.

She wasn't a pretty woman. Her hair was too dark and coarse, her face too angular and strong-featured. Her lips were narrow, proud, and contemptuous and her black eyes flashed disdain.

She said, "Men's games are little boy's games." She held the glass in her hand, high above her head.

She struck.

Thunk!

And the handle of the mug fell into her hand, waist-high.

Her knife was smaller than his, with a skinny, curved blade. The haft was a single black horn capped with a ball of silver. It lay in the bull's-eye beside the brass knife, shading it.

Silence. The roar. The laughter. The whoops. The shouts. And John Slocum's voice shouted with them. He always admired style.

Strangest of all, Arnaud, the man she had beaten, seemed as happy at her victory as if he'd won himself. He took the woman's arm and strutted her around, presenting her to the crowd for its honest admiration.

Old Murchison was hooting and hollering with everybody else, but his daughter was tugging on his sleeve. She'd had enough of the low life for one evening.

As Arnaud and his sister (for so she turned out to be) circled through the crowd like a couple in a cakewalk, Arnaud kept one eye on John Slocum. They were like two strange stud dogs, and though they never spoke and their glances never met full on, neither made a move the other missed.

Smitty saw how it was going. He went to the stairs at the back of the cantina and up to the second floor. The old belly robber took the hand of the Indian whore and said he had five dollars if she had the time. She took his five and stood beside him watching. The excitement wasn't over, not by a long shot.

John Slocum lounged against the bar. Somebody found a small squeezebox under the bar and played a couple of Spanish tunes. The musician only knew two, and when he'd exhausted his smiling, wheezing, happy repertory, he quit. Some men know their limits.

Slocum slapped two double eagles—forty dollars, gold—on the bar. "I never did see knife work like that before," he said slowly and loudly. "It was as quick as the gila monster's darting tongue." Then he added, "Drinks are one me."

In a cantina in a poor town like Seguro, free drinks are infrequent, and the bartender stared, waiting to learn if this was a wedding or a funeral or a confirmation or what. Slocum paid no further mind, sipping on his trade whiskey like it was some kind of decent-tasting liquor.

"Señors! Señoritas! Drinks for everybody. Celebrate Arnaud and Sabrina's skill with the knife. The stranger is buying everyone a drink!" The bartender did it up big, with flourishes. Another big pause because the drinkers weren't any more accustomed to generosity than the bartender was. Then the rush as everybody pressed together for their glass of cheap whiskey. "Señor!"

"*Gracias*, señor!"

"Many thanks."

To everyone's response, Slocum made one gesture: He touched the tip of his hat. He found himself looking at Arnaud and his sister. Arnaud made a little mocking bow but didn't go up for a drink. Slocum smiled, and Arnaud's smile grew as big and bright as the noonday sun. Sabrina whispered in her brother's ear, one eye on John Slocum. Arnaud shrugged her off angrily. She went to his ear again, and Slocum knew Arnaud's reluctant nod was his promise to leave the tall black-clad stranger strictly alone—no matter how much fun the fight might be.

Slocum went back to the bar. Somewhat shyly, his fellows opened conversation. Yes, it had been mighty dry lately, and yes, the winter was taking its own sweet time getting here but it can't come too late for me, no sir, I ain't no kid anymore.

"I can predict the weather with my knee," one veteran confessed.

"Do tell." John Slocum was always polite when it didn't matter.

Somebody was talking about sheep. Talking about the laurel, which poisons them dead, yes sir, twenty minutes after they been grazing on it they go belly up. One of the dark-featured men explained that wild cherry in wilt killed sheep but never bothered the mule deer who ate it without harm. The dark-faced man's English was good, his intonation was musical and fluid.

Slocum took it in. After all, his new business was sheep.

A dark-faced man was at Slocum's elbow. Arnaud was going to press his luck. A slight but discernible collective sigh went up from the others. The fun had begun.

Arnaud nodded formally to the black-clad stranger. He leaned over the bar and said, "Bring me some grappa. I don't drink this pig swill."

The bartender hastened to comply. He brought a squat bottle of a purplish whiskey and a glass.

"Bring me a glass too," Slocum said. "I'm no fonder of pig swill than this gentleman."

The bartender waited for Arnaud's nod before scuttling after the glass. Politely, Arnaud poured Slocum's drink before his own.

"Confusion to your enemies," Slocum said. Since Arnaud tossed his drink down, Slocum did the same. It burst hotter and quicker than the trade whiskey, and he had to open his mouth to let out some of the fumes. "Uh-huh," he said.

Arnaud smiled. He deliberately set one elbow on the bar. He said, "Did you know that cattlemen are the greatest liars in God's creation?" John Slocum wasn't particularly flattered being taken for a cattle-man, though he'd been one a time or two. "Do tell," he said.

"The stupid cattleman, he thinks that cows will not graze or water after sheep. South of here, where we work the big flocks, there are too few ponds to go around—we wait until the night, after all the cows have drunk, and we let our sheep drink and then we brush out the tracks with cedar bushes, and the next morning we ride into town and we hear the cowboys saying these foolish things over and over to each other. Each nods solemnly when he hears one of his cherished stupid beliefs. Oh, it makes me laugh.'' He laughed, demonstrating his foolish-cowboy laugh.

"Do tell."

"These cattlemen think they can come and harass the shepherds as they go about their daily work. It is not enough we have the wolves and the prairie fires and the poisonous plants and the lightning and the other risks. When we return to the campfire at night we find a dozen armed men waiting for us, and they say the same foolish things about sheep that we hear in the saloons. It can make me laugh." Once more he laughed to prove his point—a soundless baring of the teeth.

"You are Basque," Slocum said.

Arnaud raised one black eyebrow very high. His eyebrow was an elegant insult.

Slocum's steady gaze, waiting for the reply.

The eloquent, silent eyebrow.

" 'Course," Slocum said, "maybe you're 'shamed bein' a Basque. I wouldn't know about that." Carefully he refilled Arnaud's glass and then his own. He lifted his glass and waited. He said, "I drink to General Robert E. Lee, the most gallant commander."

In any place that size there had to be a couple of old-time Rebs, and one or two voices chimed in, "Gen'r'l Lee. Here's to him."

Arnaud raised his glass in turn. "I offer a toast to my sister Sabrina, who is the most beautiful of gentlewomen." Quickly he tossed off his own glass. "You do not drink to my sister, señor?" The warning hiss in his voice was exactly the hiss a rattlesnake makes before it starts shaking its tail.

Slocum's voice was as smooth as new cream.

"Well, sir, I'd like to correct that oversight." He wrapped one hand around the bottle and spun off the bar, so quick Arnaud didn't have time to anticipate his next move.

Sabrina was against the wall beneath the balcony. She'd separated herself from the men at the bar and the whores over her head. She tilted her head as the stranger approached. Her eyes had the same hot glitter as her brother's, but she was much less stylized than he.

"Señor," she acknowledged him, perfectly poised, perfectly neutral.

Arnaud hadn't meant the woman to be drawn into this.

Above, on the balcony, Smitty stepped behind his whore for a moment, and when he reappeared his old army holster was unbuttoned and the flap was tucked back.

"I have never seen anyone move so fast as you did, ma'am," Slocum began. He removed his hat. "Though knife work is an unusual accomplishment for a lady." He paused for her brother's angry noise, and when he heard it—that same hiss—he continued. "And such a beautiful lady at that."

Briskly, "Thank you, señor. Since we have nothing in common, nothing to speak about, perhaps you will excuse me . . ."

"Ma'am, we have some business to discuss."

Her forefinger touched her breast. "You and I? Señor, surely you have mistaken me for someone else. Judging from the bottle you have clasped in your hand, you are ready to do business with one of the girls upstairs, who will be more than glad to 'talk' with you in any position you might desire.''

Well, that broke 'em up. The crowd laughed, and the Basques banged each other on the shoulder and chattered in their strange lingo.

Slocum's smile never varied. ''I'm here to hire some herders, ma'am,'' he said.

''Herders?'' Comprehension dawned in Sabrina's face. She'd thought this man was here for the Saturday-night fights.

''Yes, ma'am. I need two Basques.''

She looked at him for the longest time. One of his hands held his hat, the other held the bottle of grappa. He should have seemed foolish. Instead, he seemed patient. She shuddered at his patience, because it reminded her of the patience of the black-winged vultures in the hot lands to the south.

''Do you prepare funerals for Basques?'' she snapped. ''You are dressed like an undertaker.''

''I surely don't hope to bury no Basques,'' he said. ''Though there'll be some buryin' work attached to the herding, should you and your brother take the job.''

She was tired of this. She looked around at the too familiar walls, the holes in the adobe where the rough rock showed through, the hard earth floor. When somebody gets cut with a knife, earth floors are easy to clean. Just scrape away the blood in the morning. ''Why not talk to my brother?'' she asked. She wondered if she was getting a headache. The black-clad man was not unhandsome. He stood over six feet, regular features, somewhat darker than most

Anglos. Dressed neatly and expensively. Soft-spoken, well-mannered.

Perhaps she was afraid of him. "Talk to Arnaud about it," she said. She meant to go, but some slight move of his stopped her.

"I can't talk to your brother about anything yet," he said.

Why did she feel a chill down her spine? Was a door open somewhere? Was there a night draft? "And why is that?"

"Because I'd have to kill him."

A hand on Slocum's shoulder. A hand spun him around. Arnaud's livid face, inches from his own. "Señor," he spat. "If you talk of killing me, do not talk to my sister. I will be glad to oblige you if there is killing to be done."

Slocum's composure never changed. His smile was slow and affable. It was the kind of a smile a farmer might wear explaining to the banker why he couldn't meet his note. "You see? That's just what I mean. Now, like I was tellin' your handsome sister . . ."

"Do not speak of my sister. Dogs like you sully my sister's name when it passes your lips."

Slocum grinned. Seguro had one big advantage over Silver City—the chance for a little light amusement on a Saturday night. He'd almost forgotten how much fun it could be. "Well now," he murmured. "You are surely ready to take an insult."

Arnaud's eyes were popping like pine resin in a hot fire. "Señor, the time for talking is done."

"You don't know the ground rules, son," Slocum said. "You think you got a bar full of your friends at your back, but that ain't so. What you got is a gunfighter name of Smitty up on that balcony behind me, and Smitty rode with Mr. Quantrill and the James boys and the Youngers, and he is a dead shot on horse or afoot.''

Smitty drew back the hammer of his revolver. He'd never used it before and it was pretty stiff, but it made the usual nasty *click click click* Slocum wanted to hear.

"So that makes us even, son. It's just you and me, belly to belly, in this little affair.'' Quick smile.

The smile was all the cue Arnaud needed. His hand flicked toward the exact spot where his knife hilt rested, and his hand was moving pretty fast, so it almost broke his fingers when he ran them into the steel barrel of Slocum's Colt. His hand jammed against the gun pressing against the middle of his diaphragm above his sash and his knife. Slocum had drawn his Colt that quick.

"You're dead,'' John Slocum said.

"No,'' a voice behind him said, "it is you who are dead.'' And Slocum felt the tip of a knife in the little hollow of his throat below his right ear. He felt the pain. He felt the tiny flow of hot blood. He froze. His gun in Arnaud's gut. Sabrina's knife where she could cut his throat in an instant. The knife pressure was quite steady, and as the nerves in his neck went numb, it seemed like some dull instrument was pressing there.

Slocum laughed. "Hell,'' he said. "Is this any way to treat a man who wants to offer you a job?''

Dead silence. The knife jiggled ever so slightly. He heard a woman's giggle. He unlatched the hammer of his Colt and holstered the weapon. The knife went away accompanied by that same giggle.

Arnaud stuck his hand out. He said, "I am Arnaud Oleacharga. I am Basque."

"John Slocum. I was born in Georgia. Once, I was out in Wyoming when the cowboys were giving trouble to the sheep people until they hired themselves a bunch of Basque shepherds. I got a little problem you could help me solve. Two weeks work. A hundred dollars a week."

Smitty put his revolver away and turned to the impassive whore standing next to him. "If I got any time left with my five dollars, we could go inside now."

And the whore, impressed at the way the staunch little man had covered the room of dangerous strangers, said, "Sure, why not?" and led Smitty to her crib.

Slocum and his new crew sat at a table in the back, and when Arnaud called for three glasses the bartender brought them in a hurry. The bartender was a happy man. A narrowly averted fight sells a lot more booze and breaks fewer glasses than a donnybrook does.

Arnaud was rubbing his hand openly. He'd half curled his hand for the haft of his knife before he ran into Slocum's pistol, and the knuckle of his fourth finger was already swelling. "*Amigo*," he said wonderingly, "where did you learn to draw a pistol like that?"

"It was Bill Hickok gave me the first lessons," Slocum said. "Hickok was fighting in Kansas, though he fought for the blue. I was just a green kid. Hickok could do stunts with his pistols you would doubt if I told you. And he was a two-handed gunfighter too. Me, I prefer the right hand.''

Sabrina poured them brimming glasses, a half inch for herself. Her hands were shaking. She'd killed wolves and bobcats with her fine Toledo knife, but she'd never come closer to killing a man. The feeling made her tremble and nauseated her.

Slocum's smile was gentle. ''Here's to you, señorita . . .''

''Sabrina Oleacharga.''

''I'm awful glad to make your acquaintance, ma'am, though you scared the tar out of me back there.''

Fiercely she said, ''I would have used the knife if you had pulled the trigger.''

''Figured you would.'' He touched below his ear where blood still oozed. ''I didn't mean to shoot Arnaud. Hell, I need him. A corpse never did me a bit of good.''

''Then why did you make a fight with him?''

''Because, señorita, him and me are too much alike. The same kind of man. If we was a little different, we could go on all our lives without causin' no harm, sayin' good morning or good afternoon as we pass by on the street. But we ain't. So we can't get along until we have a fight. I know it, and I'd venture your brother knows it too.''

Arnaud's rueful grin. ''It is true what he says. It is like two rams put into the same lot. They must fight before they know each other. Señor, you have come to Seguro just to hire two shepherds?''

So John Slocum told Arnaud about Teton Jackson and the killings he had to his credit. He spoke of the swift descent of winter in the high country north of here.

"For this fighting you pay a hundred dollars a week?"

"Yes."

"Each?"

Slocum grinned. Slowly, he nodded.

"Then you have your shepherds, señor. Me and Sabrina will move your sheep out of the highlands."

Slocum objected. He said that the job was dangerous and bloodshed was certain before it was done.

"You have seen my sister, señor." Arnaud didn't bother to conceal his pride.

"Sure. But there's all the difference in the world between tossin' a knife into a target and a man's throat." Of its own volition, Slocum's hand went up to touch the fresh wound. He winced. He nodded. "Point taken," he said. "Damned if you ain't the most dangerous lady I ever saw."

Sabrina thanked him for the compliment, but her thanks were halfhearted. Perhaps she wanted the tall gringo to think her other than dangerous. She'd seen the woman he came with. Pale, pale gringo, almost invisibly pale. What could such a strong man want with a woman like her?

"Sabrina?" Arnaud called her back from her revery. "We will leave in the morning. I will see to our horses if you can ready the dogs. We will be taking the train north, and Mr. Slocum will hire a boxcar."

Sabrina wanted to stay longer, but Slocum and Arnaud seemed hell-bent on getting through the bottle of whiskey. Once that was gone they argued solemnly over who should buy the next one, and that sort of argument isn't interesting to anyone except the drunks having it. And so, before they'd started their second bottle, Sabrina went down the street to the little house they'd inherited when their father died four years ago.

She waited a very long time for her brother to come home.

Since the dogs and the horses had to travel in a boxcar, Sabrina and Arnaud rode there too. Well, it wasn't exactly John Slocum's cup of tea—things would get rough soon enough without enduring hardships on the way—but he was no fool. He settled himself against the rough planks of the swaying boxcar and dozed.

Murchison rode in the parlor car, of course, and John Slocum wished he was with him, blowing cigar smoke in his face and drinking brandy.

The boxcar was fairly well built, and the stalls broke up the drafts, but it was October and they were climbing into the high country again. John Slocum wrapped his sheepskin closer around his body and wondered how he'd got used to being warm so quick when they'd only been in Seguro one day.

Slocum was wearing his traveling clothes. The black suit and the gold watch were locked in a horse pannier, and they'd stay there until he heard the riffle of the cards again.

His coat was heavy sheepskin that came down long enough to keep his legs dry and was split high in the back for riding. His pants were ordinary sixteen-ounce rider's denims—they'd seen some wear. His plainsman's boots were two tones (the inside of each boot bleached faster from the horse sweat than the other side from the sun).

Two .36 caliber cap-and-ball navy Colts hung at his waist. Each Colt was locked down with a hammer thong. Another pair of Colts, long-barreled Dragoons, were in saddle holsters, closed in case of bad weather.

The gear felt heavy and peculiar to his body. It was always that way for a couple of days anyway. Simple blue shirt, calico shirt, and a gray Stetson with the high horseman's crown. That air stuck between your scalp and the top of the beaver felt stayed warm in winter and slowed the sun in summertime.

Summertime. Whenever that'd come.

They accompanied a shipment of nails and farm implements, and Arnaud sat on a nail keg whittling. Of course he used his penknife. His brass-hilted knife was for serious matters. Patiently Arnaud whittled the long arm of a crucifix and cut a tiny mortise to accept the long access of the cross and the tiny tiny man carved on it. Christ's features were rough and strong. Carefully, Arnaud smoothed the arm on which he'd hang.

Sabrina sat on the cast-iron seat of a gaily painted horse-drawn Deering mower. Sabrina had her knees drawn up to her chin. Occasionally she'd drop her head into her arms, and occasionally she'd just stare. She was taking the time for dreaming.

John Slocum had a little buzz behind his eyes, and his stomach wouldn't have looked with favor on any kind of food at all, but it was one of those morning-afters that didn't feel so awful bad. Him and Arnaud had lined them up and put them away last night. The drinks had flowed free, and strangers had come up to be introduced, and he must have shaken hands with half the Basque shepherds in the state. Their high lilting language was unlike any other in the world, except for Magyar and the language of Lapland. They came to this country to work sheep, coming with a lifetime of experience herding their charges on the high rocky steeps of their barren homeland. There the shepherd would spend months out in the rough country with his flock, he and his dogs keeping the sheep from sickness and danger. Doing all the work described so brilliantly in the Twenty-third Psalm. They'd bring the animals in to lamb and sell off the full-grown yearlings, and when they marched into the high stone village behind thousands of their white-fleeced charges it was time for celebration, as if they must balance the effects of months of loneliness with a week of complete inebriation.

Arnaud and his sister had come to the end of such a week. They'd brought another man's flock down from winter pasture and had had their blowout (or at least Arnaud had had his—his sister accompanied him everywhere but wasn't much of a drinker), and now they were ready to take on this new job. It wouldn't be any harder than fighting the bears away from the flock back in the homeland they'd grown up in.

Sabrina and Mary Anne took a hearty dislike to each other right away. The two Murchisons were waiting outside Seguro's only rooming house when Slocum and the Basques stumbled into the light.

Sabrina was peeved at Arnaud and the tall stranger—one drunken celebration too many. Mary Anne made some slighting remark—she was glad Slocum had hired two *men* for the difficult and dangerous job before them. Well, Sabrina's face went scarlet before Mary Anne finished talking.

Murchison said, "Excuse me, ma'am," and tipped his hat, apologizing for his daughter. He didn't rise, because he didn't have any strength in his legs this morning. Funny how the strength came and went.

"I'm so sorry," Mary Anne said, though she wasn't.

"Yes, señorita," Sabrina replied quietly. "You are very womanly."

It was Mary Anne's turn to color at a remark that should have been a compliment but surely wasn't intended to be.

"I try to keep myself feminine," she replied. "The boys like it that way."

"The boys, señorita? And the men, what do they like?"

That was how it went that morning—the two of them taking potshots at each other while they got their gear together and Slocum bought horses.

Smitty traveled with Murchison, helping him walk, getting him glasses of water; once or twice he wiped the sick man's pale brow.

The Basques had their own horses, two each—short-legged, big-barreled animals with tremendous chests on them. They wouldn't make much speed, but they'd carry a load all day without complaint; and they'd draw a wagon out of a stream or carry a rider with equal aplomb. They were mountain horses. Slocum found a tall black mare with a pretty good turn of speed and the spirit Slocum liked. She was tall in the legs and graceful as an Arabian. His packhorse was a tough grullo mustang, hammer-headed, thick across the shoulders, and heavy-muscled. The mustang had a mean eye and tried to take a nip out of Slocum's arm, so he belted it a good one just to convince the horse of his new and different relationship. Sixty dollars bought the black and forty more took the mustang. They would have cost twice that figure, but the man selling the horses was some kind of cousin to Arnaud.

Arnaud was worse hung over than Slocum. Probably that was why he was carving on his crucifix. A hangover can do that sort of thing to a man.

Slocum's watchful gaze, Arnaud's sad careful face, his sister's dreamy eyes.

One of the horses stamped in its stall and a dog looked up. Four dogs lay around Arnaud. Two of them were coupled together with a short length of chain and a lead. The other two wore no collars and lay free.

Two bony, curly-haired white dogs with an unpronounceable Basque name. Slocum had no luck getting his tongue around the syllables. Sabrina laughed and said, "Just call them Jolla and Neva. They are the dogs that kill bears."

They had less jaw than a crocodile but not much less. They carried no weight on their body except the powerful hindquarters and the massive heads. The two dogs slept peacefully, placid among the people they saw as family, but had a stranger come into that boxcar at any of the watering stops the chain would have been necessary. They were trained to guard. The other two dogs were smaller and fluffy, and Slocum thought they looked just like the dogs old ladies kept, getting fat before the fire. They were quite affectionate, and both always had some part of their body touching Arnaud's legs. These were the herding dogs.

Slocum got out at the next stop and splashed water on his face and hands and dried himself on his shirt sleeve. He touched the faint stubble on his face. His facial hair was very black, and by tomorrow he'd look pretty rough. He stretched. Damn! It felt pretty good being on the trail again.

Maybe it had been a mistake staying at Silver City so long. Maybe so, maybe not. If he was to spend time recounting his mistakes he wouldn't have time for anything else.

The sun was bright and cold and very high. The roadbed was sharp under his boots. The locomotives chuffed a column of pure white smoke into the air. It'd darken when they poured the coal to her, and that's when the cinders fell.

Other passengers took their own constitutionals beside the tracks, and there was a slight procession of men and boys behind the tower where a circle of dead grass marked the place to make water.

Slocum nodded to a few men who nodded back. He said "How do" to a small girl who disappeared behind her mother's skirt. He heard the most god-awful snarling he had ever heard in his life. Yips and growls that set his heart to pounding before he began to run.

Mary Anne was at the boxcar door leaning against the wood, white as a sheet. Basque commands rang out, and the growls slowed to a constant low *grrr*. Arnaud popped his head out. "I am sorry, señorita," he said. "The dogs were startled when you appeared so suddenly."

Mary Anne stopped being scared and started to get mad, and she picked John Slocum as prime target. "If you had been riding with Daddy and me, this never would have happened!"

Slocum said, "You ain't hurt," which was not perhaps the most diplomatic thing he could have said.

She stamped her feet. She looked daggers. She said, quite distinctly, "You can always find a gentleman among his peers."

Slocum's grin was quite good-natured. "I never did claim to be one of those, Mary Anne."

She said some more harsh words and turned on her heel and went back to the parlor car.

Slocum wanted to talk to Murchison and Smitty.

Item: Teton Jackson was willing to kill to keep Murchison's woolies on the mountain.

Item: Jackson had traveled with three other badhats.

Item: Jackson's bunch hung out at a roadhouse that had come to be known as Robber's Roost, which wasn't the sort of name that attracted tourists or drummers but might seem inviting to men who rode the Hoot Owl Trail. How many men could Jackson count on?

Well, Slocum would have to wait to ask his questions. Give her time and Mary Anne would cool off. He scratched his head. The brakeman and conductor signaled back and forth, and the locomotive released a cloud of steam.

Arnaud took Slocum's hand to pull him aboard.

"Thank you, amigo."

Arnaud laughed. "She is quite a one, eh, the *rubia*?"

"You bet."

"When the dogs jumped at her, I expected her to faint or make water, but she did not. She is harder than she looks, that one."

Slocum thought about the cold-blooded bargain the woman had struck with him: a night of lovemaking in trade for dangerous work. He didn't say anything.

Sabrina rattled something off.

"What was that?"

Arnaud adopted his solemn expression. "Señor Slocum, there are words that are too awful to hear in any language. My sister does not care for the *rubia*. My sister will tear her tongue out if she continues to insult her." He shrugged. He whittled a thin piece of wood off the butt end of his crucifix. "She'll do it too," he added.

Besides the knives they carried, both Basques owned shotguns of a curious European design. Above the twin barrels each had a third barrel that was rifled and took a slug. The weapons could be used on birds or game, or, as Arnaud put it, "They kill any wild thing that walks or flies." Slocum thought the three-barreled guns were an interesting idea. He'd seen plenty of multi-barreled revolvers (the eight-barrel Allen pepperbox was the drummer's favorite), but he'd never seen a multi-barreled shoulder weapon before.

That night they ate their supper on the train. Murchison and his haughty daughter were served by a white-coated porter: fine china and linen set out on little tables he drew up beside them. Slocum and the

Basques ate beef jerky and half a loaf of round bread with a packing case as their table and the floor of the car for seats. Probably the three in the boxcar enjoyed their meal more, and they certainly slept just as soundly.

Morning found them back in Soda Springs. Murchison was close to the end of his rope. The familiarity of the town that had served him and his ranch for thirty years knocked the stuffing right out of him. Of course, there were any number of people waiting for the morning train, and plenty of them knew old J.D. Murchison, and every darn one of them told him how awful he looked. They didn't help.

At six-thirty in the morning the train created all the human activity in the tiny town of Soda Springs. John Slocum got the grocer to open the Soda Springs Mercantile by banging on the back door until that worthy came down to open up for them.

Smitty bought foodstuffs. Slocum added grain, equipage for the horses, and guns and ammunition. Over protests he bought Colts for Arnaud and his sister. He bought a lighter Smith & Wesson for Mary Anne, though she swore she'd never use it.

"If they're coming for you and the rest of us are dead, you might change your mind," Slocum said.

She took it.

The town was completely awake when they rode east out of Soda Springs on the stage road. Slocum rode out front; a half mile behind followed the buckboard, which was loaded like a cook wagon. Murchison rode with both hands curled over the seat, white as winter-killed corn.

His face was so close to death it was painful to

look at. Something must have gone wrong with the blood supply to his lips, because they were cracked and sore, and his tongue lapped at them, tired and dry.

Smitty drove carefully. If there was a smooth path between the ruts, Smitty found it. It didn't make too much difference by now.

Mary Anne rode behind the buckboard, and what she thought shall remain locked forever inside her pretty little head.

Arnaud and his sister rode drag, bringing up the rear.

From time to time a little breeze kicked up dust devils on the dry road. The brush was gray, and the high plains seemed to go on forever. They saw no other travelers, though they rode until noon, stopped for an hour to rest the horses, and rode another half hour to the turnoff for Jackson's roadhouse.

The brushy lane cut off at a diagonal. It was not much traveled, but Teton Jackson had probably never meant his place to be convenient.

Five miles, ten. The lane wandered. It was easy enough on the level, but when the lane took to a dry streambed the buckboard heaved and lurched despite Smitty's very best efforts. Murchison swayed in the seat.

The day was warm enough when they stayed on open ground, but it got chilly as soon as they passed into the the pine trees, with their depths and chirpings and strange cool silences.

Scared up a couple of camp robbers and three magpies. Slocum noted an osprey perched on a dead branch above the dry creek.

The road was almost too narrow for the buckboard to pass between the trees. The shadows grew long. Smitty wouldn't look at Murchison's face anymore. He checked his boss with a glance at his white-knuckled hands. When those hands went slack it'd be time to stop.

Jackson's roadhouse was set in a narrow canyon. The walls of the canyon were pretty steep, rough talus at the base giving way to broken cliffs.

John Slocum stopped within the trees and gave the place the once-over.

The roadhouse was a low, cedar-shaked log house. Couldn't have been more than a couple of rooms with a loft upstairs. A corral in front. Slocum heard a yell from the building. A man stumbled outside and took a piss in the same yard where the horses took theirs.

Inside, a shouted curse. Without turning loose of himself, the man turned his head and hollered his own curse right back.

Slocum talked it over with the others. Maybe they could pull Mr. Treton Jackson's stinger before he knew everything wasn't going his way.

Arnaud and Sabrina were willing to go along with Slocum's ideas, and Smitty was game. Mary Anne didn't want to have anything to do with it. Slocum had meant to leave Murchison out, but inside his dying body a spark fanned into flame and forced the life back into his eyes. "All your life, Mary Anne," he said, "you've had things given to you. This time you're gonna have to fight for them same as everybody else."

"Those corral poles ain't much protection," Slocum said, "but they ain't gonna be expecting you, and they'll be mad as hornets."

"Get on with it," Murchison said shortly. He didn't have enough life left to be long.

Slocum pulled his Colts and checked the caps for dust and moisture. Okay. He removed one of his saddle pistols and stuck that behind his belt in the small of his back. His light denim jacket covered it pretty good.

Smitty imitated the process with his J.W. Dance. He sighed. He said, "I sure hope I can hit something with this."

"Hold it with both hands. Keep both eyes open. Put your pills into the man's stomach." Slocum left his jacket unbuttoned and the hammer thongs unhooked.

A little wind came out of the mouth of the canyon and spooked the horses. If the canyon widened farther along, and if it held a little water, it would be a wonderful place to hold stolen cattle. The roadhouse at the mouth of the canyon would be the cork in the bottle.

Slocum set Mary Anne Murchison just where he wanted her: beside the corral's largest gatepost.

She eyed the ground with distaste, though it was bare and hard with no fresh piles of manure. "Must I?"

"If you got to do it later, you might as well do it now," Slocum explained patiently. He figured to put her down low and hoped she'd stay there.

Slocum helped J.D. Murchison lie down. His daughter flounced and kicked up like a broody hen. Slocum handed them the three-barreled shotguns and cautioned them. "Now don't pull the triggers at once. You won't do much good that way, and the kick will knock you into the middle of next week. And Mary Anne?''

"Yes?''

"If you decide to get up because you're uncomfortable or got an itch or are awful damn scared, why then, our plan ain't gonna work and we're all dead. They'd particularly like to get you, because they probably ain't had themselves a woman like you in their misspent lives. You think about that when you get nervous or itchy and want to get comfortable, hear?''

She made a face.

Slocum stationed Smitty across the corral. "I gave the shotguns to the Murchisons because I figured they couldn't hit nothing without them. I want a little more from you, Smitty. You got your J.W. Dance. You take this long gun—it's a Henry .44. If you don't empty a few saddles, well then, Smitty, you ain't worth a damn."

Smitty grinned.

Slocum took a deep breath and met Arnaud's eyes. The madness of battle glowed in those eyes, hot as his own. Sabrina's dark eyes held sadness.

Slocum said, "They are wolves, Sabrina, and they will kill your flock."

"Ah yes," she said. "And they are men, too, are they not? And it is a little sad."

"Maybe it's a little bit funny."

She rubbed her nose. The Colt she wore inside her short jacket was an unfamiliar weight. She checked her saddle hoslters once more, wedging one flap under the leading edge of her saddle. That'd hold it.

They made their tiny moves and last-minute adjustments. Okay. They passed through the corral where their friends were stationed. Slocum stopped his horse at the hitchrail but didn't tie up. He ground-hitched instead, because coming out fast, they might save half a second that way. The planks of the porch echoed under his boots—*boom, boom*—and he figured the boys inside had already heard him.

With the Basques at his back, he pushed the door open.

It was as dark as a rathole inside. Side windows let in some light, and a bigger window faced the canyon wall, fifty feet out back. The privy was out back too.

Faces: young faces, older faces. Male faces all. All hard faces.

"Afternoon," Slocum said amiably enough. "I was hopin' this was Mr. Teton Jackson's roadhouse."

"Might be," somebody growled. "Might not be too. Depends who's asking."

God, it smelled awful in there. Slocum had smelled bear caves with a milder stench.

John Slocum had lived as long as he had because he was perfectly willing to die. His humanity dropped off him like a cocoon and revealed him as he was: new, fresh, and murderous. He smiled. "My handle's Slocum. That's John Slocum, lately of Missouri and Kansas and Silver City."

Everybody in that bunch wouldn't know him. He waited for the whispers and they came too. "He rode with Quantrill." "Cole Younger's pal." "Killed four vigilantes up in Montana." "John Slocum . . ."

Sabrina stepped inside on his right. Arnaud took the left. Slocum counted the house. Made it twenty—no, twenty-four men including the barman and the two in the corner. The barman's lower lip was cleft so severely it revealed two front teeth. A scar wound down his left cheek, and somebody had bounced a tomahawk off his skull once—a groove that made a second part in his greasy brown hair. He tried a smile, and it was a mighty poor attempt. "Yeah. This is Jackson's. Ol' Teton's not here today if that's who you're looking for."

"Ain't lookin' for nobody in particular. Not today."

John Slocum let his last two words hang in the air like a sword suspended by a thread. He left no doubt that some day he might be coming back and the man he was looking for should update his will. It's wonderful what a couple of words can suggest.

"Teton, he ain't here," Cleft Lip repeated.

"Uh-huh. How about his pals? I expect some of you will be his riding partners."

Men looked everywhere trying to find the elusive parties John Sloucm sought. It was odd to see them put on their "Who me?" expressions; they were not a crowd of innocents. If every crime they'd done could speak, the room would be screaming and begging and crying for pity and forgiveness. The young faces and the old faces had one thing in common: They had lain down with pure evil a time or two. Slocum saw expressionless faces with tight and guarded eyes. He saw mouths that were slack-jawed and floppy and would have half talked a man's ear off. He saw young men and one or two men in their sixties.

They carried bowie knives and Arkansas toothpicks. They carried Colts, Remingtons, derringers, Smith &

Wessons, and several had shotguns in their hands. The twenty-odd men in that room had enough weapons for a company of Union cavalry—and, no doubt, more weapons with their horses. They were cow thieves, horse thieves, killers, rapists, bank robbers and road agents. The best man among them was probably the cleft-lipped barman, and he'd killed his own wife and her two little babies before he came out west. Slowly he said, "Depends who you mean. There ain't a man here who's Teton Jackson's enemy." He left it that way, giving Slocum plenty of room to declare himself.

Arnaud and Sabrina had stepped away from Slocum. One of the drunks in the back woke up. "What the hell's going on?" he demanded.

Somebody shushed him. Men shifted slightly so their weapons were handier.

"Well, friend?" the barman demanded.

Slocum's grin was dazzling. Might as well die for a sheep as a lamb. "I have come here to tell Teton Jackson that we're gonna take the Muleshoe sheep down off the mountain. Several weeks ago, Mr. Jackson and Mr. Smart and Mr. Butch and some other hardcase, they killed a man up there. Jackson said the sheep were to stay where they are. They ain't."

Silence while the men in the roadhouse digested what Slocum had said. Some men rode often with Jackson, some rarely, and for some, Jackson's friendship was no more important than a safe place to stay along the Hoot Owl Trail.

Slowly the barman spoke. "I heard something about that little affair. I heard that sheep was grazing where cows used to graze.'' He paused, searching for words. "Damn woolies!''

In a very few seconds the doorway of this room was going to be occupied with flying lead. The odds were fair to poor. Arnaud walked right up to the bar. Roughly he shoved two badhats aside. "Whiskey,'' he said. "I don't particularly want a fight right now. I want a whiskey.''

When the barman's jaw dropped, he looked like an astonished woodchuck. Automatically his hand groped for the bottle behind him. He checked his move. "We don't serve greasers in here,'' he sneered. Perhaps half the men in the room were mixed blood—breeds, Spanish, and Indians. Nobody took offense at the bartender's words. His insult was directional.

"I'd sure like to serve something to *her*,'' one loafer laughed. Big man. Long white hair and muscles gone slack with age. He carried a nickle-plated pistol in a chest holster. He stepped toward Sabrina. "Damned if I couldn't serve her something,'' he said. "I ain't seen nothin' . . . Come inside here, honey, where we can get a good look at you. Damn! With that sun in my eyes I didn't know you was even a woman.''

John Slocum spoke real quick—a trifle too quick. "I think you got us wrong,'' he said. "We're not here for trouble.''

That stopped the action, because if these three weren't here for trouble, what the hell were they doing here? Jackson's roadhouse didn't get many tourists.

White Hair stopped his advance.

"If you ain't here for trouble, it seems to me, you run into a passel of it."

Slocum's face got quite nervous. His hands stayed away from his holsters. "No 'fense meant," he said.

The barman grinned like a wolf.

White Hair grinned like a shark.

Everybody relaxed. Hell, this might turn out to be fun.

"Ol' Teton's out in the woods," the barman said, and laughed, because whenever Jackson went on a rustling expedition he said he was going "out in the woods," and it had become a joke among them.

Some others laughed. The barman came around the bar, rubbing his hands on his pants. He wanted to get a better look at this woman. With the door open, her features blurred, and he couldn't tell whether she was pretty or not. Didn't matter so much. Last woman he'd had was a squaw in a teepee outside Fort Trumbull. She had been ugly, but inside she had been warm enough. Like a wild animal, he sensed the weakness in John Slocum's trembling hands and worried voice, and he felt nothing but contempt for this weakling who'd come right into the midst of his enemies and made a play that wasn't strong enough to stick. He'd have the woman before the day was out, and he'd get his hands bloody doing it.

The barman was feeling pretty confident when he died.

Arnaud's knife took him in the kidneys, and he felt that surge of pain and his lights went out.

Whitey was out in front. The woman moved, and Whitey put his hands up to his neck and made an awful sound. He took a step back with his right foot, moving quite normally, and his wrists were darkening with the blood that surged out of the slash where his Adam's apple had been, where the black hilt of Sabrina's knife gleamed. That quick she reclaimed her weapon. She kept it loose in her hands, ready to fly again.

The barman hit the floor and made it bounce. Whitey stumbled rubber-legged to the wall hugging the rough wood as he slumped into death.

"Never did pay to insult a lady," Slocum said cheerfully. "We came up here to warn you boys that it's hands off the Muleshoe stock. I had meant to kill me a few snakes in this den, Teton Jackson among them. But he ain't here, you say . . ."

Sabrina hurried outside. Arnaud bent and retrieved his blade. He followed his sister.

"So," Slocum concluded, "I guess I got to kill whichever of you snakes is handiest. Fill your hands!"

It might have been avoided. If, among that bunch of scoundrels and backshooters, nobody had reached for his weapon, John Slocum would have backed out of the roadhouse and kicked the door shut behind him.

But thieves or not, there weren't too many cowards in Robber's Roost that day, and men reached for their iron. They were off balance and slow. The two bodies on the floor didn't make them move any faster, and John Slocum emptied his right-hand Colt, five cylinders loaded and primed, before he executed a textbook border shift. The steady roar of his pistol, the slap as the left-hand pistol replaced the empty. Another steady roar and he was backing out of the doorway and his left hand went behind his back for his third pistol and he kicked the door shut.

He dove for his horse as gouts of wood jumped out of the door behind him.

Inside it was carnage. Carnage of men dying, carnage of men pushing past the falling bodies for a clear shot, charging to the door, as angry as a yellowjacket nest kicked by a cow.

A half dozen men hit the door from the inside, knocked it open, knocked it off the top of its leather hinges so the door hung askew. They swarmed onto the porch, their eyes red with gunpowder sting, half deafened by the roar of guns inside the closed room, and one thought on each man's mind: to get in one clean shot at that black-haired sonofabitch, to bring him down and the two greasers, too.

They came from darkness into full sunlight, and at this altitude the sunlight was awful damn bright. Slocum and his companions were flogging their horses, riding like banshees.

Jackson's bunch booted their horses into a crow-hopping run after the fleeing party. Just as their horses settled down for the run—just as they came hurtling toward the corral gate, a woman in a pretty blue riding outfit stood up with a huge scattergun in her hands, closed her eyes, and fired.

One barrel. A pause before her numb finger found the second trigger and the shotgun blasted again. It was point-blank: One man went off his horse with his damn arm shot off below the elbow; the second charge Mary Anne fired ruined a rider's head and came within a shoelace of severing it completely.

Her father fired. Smitty had his Colt pointed just

as instructed. Fired one shot. Wait for the smoke to clear. Ah, another target, that rider on the mustang over by the corral corner. There. A shot. Took him right out of the saddle, neat as you please.

Slocum and the two Basques came back straight at the corral, riding as hard as they'd fled, and all three worked their saddle guns, Slocum's pistols sparkling like the Fourth of July. He rode with his reins between his teeth and standing in the stirrups. One of his bullets hurled a man back into the porch wall and another took off a man's ear as neat as a surgeon.

Mounted men in the corral—six of them. They all got shot pretty bad except for one lucky soul who jumped his horse over the corral rails and furiously made tracks down the canyon.

Two men on the porch still firing, and, hell, this wasn't their fight! They hadn't asked for it! They threw up their hands.

Slocum and the Basques drew up. Five bodies in the yard, another two on the porch. Somebody inside was screaming, several cursing.

Smitty put his pistol back into its holster and closed the leather flap. He was smiling.

The two prisoners had their hands stuck high. They said this was none of their fight.

Mary Anne helped Murchison through the corral. It was hard going because several horses were quite skittish, and their temper wasn't improved when Murchison slapped at them with the butt of the shotgun.

Slocum marveled at where it came from: this strength in a dying man.

"Mount up," Slocum said to Smitty. "There's a

few boys inside that hellhole. We pushed them around a bit, but they won't stay quiet forever."

Smitty mounted. He was proud of himself, and it showed in his carriage and his face.

At her father's orders, Mary Anne went for the buckboard. "Damn it, girl! I can stand up. I can stand up!" And for the moment, he could. He marched up and confronted the two prisoners on the porch.

"You held up my sheep," he said. "You killed one of my riders."

"Oh no, mister. We never done that. It was Teton Jackson did that little piece of business. We was just ridin' through here. We got honest jobs down in Utah."

Murchison didn't turn his head. "Slocum!" he yelled, "Do you believe them?"

Slocum looked them over. He didn't know either of them, and he was sick of killing. His temper was down and his stomach unsettled—just like always after the shooting was done. "Sure," he said. "It might be like they say."

Murchison leveled his shotgun. He said, "I'm a dying man. Keep hell warm for me."

And with both barrels he sent them there.

5

Slocum had no appetite though there wasn't a thing wrong with Smitty's grub. "John," Smitty said, "you just try one of these here pieces of deer meat. I got it undercooked, just how you like it."

Before the shoot-up Slocum had been "Mr. Slocum" to Smitty. Nothing gets you on a first-name basis faster than blood you've shed.

Murchison's health had gone back on him, retreated inside the body to save itself for later. He lay right beside the fire, propped up against a saddle and covered with blankets, and still his face was gray and his teeth chattered when he tried to speak.

The two Basques stayed by themselves, camped a little farther up the hill from the spring they'd selected for that night's resting spot—two hours north and west of Teton Jackson's roadhouse.

Smitty was pretty smug. He made a big production of oiling and cleaning his revolver, and he cleaned the two Basques' shotguns for good measure. Smitty acted like a man who, after long delay, had come into his own.

Slocum took a cup of water through the lengthening shadows to the greasy hummock where Arnaud and Sabrina sat, side by side, equally pensive.

Slocum waited for Arnaud's gesture before he hunkered down. He broke off a stalk of broom sage and sucked on it thoughtfully.

After a very long time Sabrina said, "He was my first one. Killing him was not like killing a wolf."

"I reckon not," Slocum said. "I guess if it ever got real easy to kill a man, we wouldn't be no different from the wolves—pure wild creatures."

Coming from a man whose terrible pistols had killed until the floors ran red that very afternoon, the remark surprised her. She didn't know anyone more wolflike than this tall dark-haired gunman, and she bit her tongue so she wouldn't say so. "I am a shepherd. I take care of sheep. It is my work—what I do," she said.

"Yeah? I was a saloonkeeper a week ago. Nice place. Long bar. Big grizzly head on the wall. I don't believe I'll ever forget how that grizzly head looked."

"You were a man of property?" her brother asked.

"Don't be so damned surprised," Slocum returned. "Hell, any of us can become anything—and sometimes the becoming takes place in the blink of an eye. I been a farmer, a prospector, a gambler. Now I'm a trail boss for woolies."

"I am sorry, señor," Sabrina said softly. "I think my brother did not mean to accuse you of being too comfortable with killing."

"Yeah." Slocum spat out the broom sage. "Well, one way or another, I seem to get enough of it done." He thought about the bottle in his saddlebags and decided no. One thing he had had enough of for one day was meanness. No sense following a mean fight with a mean drunk. He leaned against his saddle and watched the horses graze and thought how Mr. Whitman, the poet, would have enjoyed seeing them, grazing the last of the lush grass beside a pool that probably had some mineral in it because it was a strange milky green color.

It was the most beautiful country ever given to man. *Too bad,* Slocum thought, *we had to bloody it up*.

He could have been kinder when Mary Anne Murchison came to stand awkwardly beside him, but he wasn't feeling like he had too much left for anyone right then—and not particularly her.

She sat down without an invitation. She put her soft hand on his arm.

He didn't want it, but wouldn't push it away.

"John . . . ?"

He sighed. "Hello, Mary Anne. How's your father feeling?"

"No change. I don't know whether he'll make it through the night. John, I'm going to be very lonely when he . . . uh, goes."

"Expect you will."

"It's a tremendous ranch, John. Muleshoe has hayfields that'll feed eight thousand sheep or fifteen hundred cows, no matter how rough the winter is. There are barns for the hay and a big stone and log ranchhouse. We've got all the mineral rights, and there are streams in the south part where prospectors found color."

"Sounds nice." His voice was uncaring.

"John, don't make me ask."

"Mary Anne, don't ask. You want to split the blanket with me, well then, I ain't made of stone and you are a fine and handsome woman.'' For the first time he raised his eyes to hers. ''But you and me ain't no more suited for each other than a cat and a dog. We'd never work in tandem. We see things too different. We're pals for tonight if you want, but that's all I got to offer.''

Her lower lip trembled. ''John . . . I was very, very scared today.''

''I reckon you were.''

''Couldn't I . . . couldn't we . . .''

Another sigh. ''Mary Anne, get your spare saddle blanket and pull it up here beside me. Smitty'll look after your father tonight, and you watchin' him ain't gonna make him live ten seconds longer.''

She brought her blanket. She brought tomorrow's clothes out of the pack and tonight's toiletries. She went down to the spring and washed her face and her arms and combed out her long yellow hair. She made quite a production out of it, and while she was preparing herself, her gallant knight was dozing, dressed except for his boots. His socks had a couple of holes, so his big toes poked through.

She shook her head. She was set on her purpose, but Mary Anne Murchison was annoyed enough to prod Slocum awake with one of her pointy-toed boots.

''A gentleman never falls asleep on a lady,'' she complained.

''Maybe so. But we ain't them.'' He pulled his socks off and rolled his shirt over his broad shoulders. It gave her the shivers—the sight of the power in his back. And at once she was ready for love. ''John?'' she croaked.

He hunched himself out of his pants and scooted under the blankets.

A horse whinnied. A nightbird set to calling. The moon was high in the sky.

She looked around quick before shedding her own outfit, because God knows she didn't want Smitty seeing her, or that Arnaud with his crazy eyes. A man who'd use a knife would do most anything. She shivered against Slocum's back. Her bristly pubes brushed against his buttocks and her knees fit into the back of his. "John," she whispered. She reached around and found his manhood, and it was hard and ready. "You said you weren't made of stone, John." She giggled. "I've got something in my hand that feels otherwise."

He turned—almost whirled around—and his face was black with his anger, and when his mouth found hers it was like rape. He drew on her, drew her out, and she was shuddering from his kisses alone. Her knees flopped wide, helpless, like they were drawing a lover in, before he stabbed into her. She said, "Oh." She put her fist in her mouth and bit down hard, because her body was jumping with his, against his, in counterpoint, and she was afraid she'd start singing.

Her fingers dug into his back until he felt her nails puncture flesh. The hot blood ran over her fingers, and she took one finger and stuck it into her mouth and tasted his blood, so sour, so sweet. Licking her fingers kept her happy as she came and came and came.

He rolled off her, exhausted and used.

She curled away from him. Neither felt any urge to

touch or talk. They didn't have that kind of relationship.

He slept hard that night, with the customary horrid dreams. Faces appeared to him; some of them were men he'd gunned, and some were the faces of men he'd just known; some were friends. They had death in common. Several of them motioned John Slocum closer, hoping he'd join up.

He awoke covered with sweat and alone. The surface of his black wool blanket was slightly frosted, and the nearby pool steamed like a hot spring.

He could hear the pop of grease from Smitty's frying pan and the coffee bubbling away in the old blue enamel coffeepot. Another day. Another chance.

He pulled clean clothes out of his saddlebags. His shirt was spattered with bloodstains, and the cuff of his pant leg was daubed with red. They'd make rags; he'd never wear them again.

Wrapped in his blanket, with his gear tucked awkwardly under his arm, John Slocum barefooted through the frosty grass to the edge of the pool. He whooped and launched himself like a damn fool kid right into that misty blue-green water, five thousand feet up in the foothills of the Rocky Mountains, November of the year.

As the water streamed past his astonished eyes, his body cramped and sent one urgent frozen signal to his brain. He burst out of the water like a seal and dug in his arms for the quick trip to shore. Knee deep, he lathered himself, soap over his goose-pimpled skin, soaping quick. His scrotum was drawn up and his cock small. He hurried that soap and clamped his eyes shut and made another dive into that icy water, holding his breath, spinning and writhing underwater to rinse himself.

He dried himself on his old shirt and hurried into his fresh clothes, his teeth chattering like they might chip.

"Well, John," Smitty remarked, "you do look refreshed, but I don't know how you could go in water like that. Catch your death from fool tricks like that."

"Uh-huh. What you cookin'? How's Murchison?"

"About the same. He slept most of the night and he's got a little more color, but this is one sickness he ain't gonna get well from."

"That's ham and eggs and biscuits. Damn, I'm hungry."

"Nobody ate a thing last night. I'm used to it. Quantrill's men came back from fighting and they never wanted nothin' to eat neither. They couldn't get enough of drink, but they never wanted no food in their belly."

"Yeah. I know."

"That's right! John, strike me dead if I hadn't forgot you rode with us in those days, I . . ."

"If you was to forget, it wouldn't bother me none." Slocum spooned eggs onto his tin plate. Fresh eggs were a real luxury at a chuck wagon. He took his plate and cup where nobody would bother him. He thought about Teton Jackson's pals and what they'd be up to. He sipped on Smitty's scalding hot coffee.

Everybody took their own breakfast (Mary Anne fed old Murchison with a spoon), and everybody saw to their own horses. These animals might spell the difference between life and death soon, and everybody wanted his in top condition.

Arnaud exercised his dogs, disappearing in the woods with the four of them. The long-haired guard dogs raced on ahead, fleet as greyhounds, and the smaller herding dogs bounced through the woods, sniffing everything, circling constantly to check with Arnaud.

They were rolling before the sun had got full up, just forty minutes after John Slocum first rolled out of his blankets. Arnaud rode beside Slocum.

"They will come after us, yes?"

"I reckon they'll get to their boss. Once they hook up with him and the unbloodied ones, they'll come riding after us."

"Still, we hurt them, yes?"

"I figure we shaded the odds a bit in our favor."

"How far do we travel today?"

"We ought to find those woolies before nightfall. We're near to the Owyhee Trail."

Murchison lay in the back of the buckboard. He no longer had the strength to hang onto the seat. Slocum didn't feel much sympathy. Murchison's shooting two unarmed men had lowered him considerably in Slocum's regard.

The Owyhee Trail was narrow and unbelievably rough. The hooves of thousands of cattle had pounded the trail soft and dusty or soft and muddy, depending on where it ran.

Slocum whistled. He lifted his Stetson and ran his hand through his hair.

Arnaud said there were very many cows, and John Slocum agreed. "I expect that Teton Jackson was driving a herd along here. I expect he didn't want no interruptions with a herd this big.''

"Smitty told me how this trail connects to a shipping town.''

"Mr. Jackson looks to be a rich man. And these damn tracks are fresh. If they was made earlier than yesterday morning, I miss my guess. Look at those droppings. They ain't got all the way hard as yet.''

"How far to his destination?''

"Wyoming is two days from here, cow speed. Two days if nothing goes haywire.''

"Jackson's boys will know where they're heading. They'll join up with them in Wyoming.''

"Them or a couple messengers. Now, I don't know how old Jackson's gonna like bein' stung. He might decide to stay in Wyoming and give us a miss. Maybe he won't have stomach for a fight.''

"That is wishful thinking, my friend.''

Slocum laughed. "Yeah. Otherwise we wouldn't be payin' a couple tough Basques just to push a bunch of sheep around.''

There was no way the buckboard could avoid the bumps and ruts. Along about eleven, Slocum tied up to the buckboard and crouched in the back above the dying rancher. Murchison's lips found Slocum's name but were unable to utter it. His eyes were hot and bright as a boy's.

"Don't you worry, pal,'' Slocum said. "Before this trip's done, we'll find something more for you to do. You'll have all the killing you can stomach.''

Murchison's smile was ghastly, and the hand that touched Slocum's sleeve was skeletal and frail.

No sounds except the ravens chattering in the woods

and the clomp and squeek and clatter of their passage. The sun made its indifferent passage. Slocum took the point again.

Nobody talked to each other. Every rider rode alone. Occasionally Smitty glanced back to see if his passenger was still breathing. Occasionally the Basques leaned together and spoke in their quick musical tongue.

Slocum couldn't help thinking about Mary Anne's offer. One of the biggest spreads in the territory, already stocked with animals, fenced, ready to go. He thought about Mary Anne Murchison. He'd heard of men who married for money and always thought it was peculiar. What could money buy? A full-stocked ranch in this beautiful country. So what if Mary Anne made his hair stand on end? So what if every sexual encounter they'd had had been a bargain?

She was a lovely and cultivated woman. She'd been educated back east. He made a point of falling back to ride beside her. He asked her if she'd ever read any of Mr. Whitman, and she said no she hadn't, that Mr. Whitman's poems were scandalous, unfitting for a young girl's shell-pink ears.

"I see." He did, too. He went back on the point, where he could ride by himself.

Though the chill got sharper the higher they climbed, it was a beautiful vasty clear western day, and the foliage flamed autumn colors along the draws and ravines. The pine forest gave way to the steeper slopes, and the mountain peaks gleamed, though Slocum knew it'd be four days to their summits. And that'd be next spring. He could see where there had been new snowfalls on the peaks.

The horses picked along where the trail clung to the steep slopes, and Smitty turned when the buckboard took a particularly savage lurch. The boss surprised him. "Help me out of here," he gasped. "This damn wagon'll be the death of me. My head's swimmin' now. Put me up on the box, and if I fall off, you just leave me. I'd rather be dead than banged around anymore."

Smitty made a dry camp, before noon, perched on the edge of a boulder-strewn slope. The slope was full of deer beds and the smell of the low-growing spearmint plants.

It was biscuits and ham, and water from the canteens, but the sun was so strong up here that a man had to squint unless he kept his hat pulled down. By all rights the altitude should have killed Murchison, but instead it made him bloom. The thin air that should have starved his lungs pumped them with life, and the sun that should have driven him to the earth pulled him up instead. He felt, if not well, at least better than two days ago. He ate, working the dry ham down his throat with swallows of tepid, metallic water.

Just a thousand yards farther on, the trail forked. Teton Jackson's cows took the south fork, meandering over a scrubby hogback and dipping out of sight toward Wyoming.

The upper trail led to the sheep.

"You go on," Slocum said. "I'll be along directly." He stayed behind to prowl the trail junction. The trail broke on the prow of a steep piece of granite sixty feet high from crown to base. Scrubby row of cedars up top.

Slocum took the long way around to examine the rocky prow that overlooked both trails. He could see more of Jackson's cow trail up here, could see a couple more turns it made. Jackson could get here as early as Sunday morning if Slocum's calculations were right (and if today was Wednesday instead of Monday or Tuesday last week). Four days from now they had better be beyond this point heading direct for Muleshoe or Jackson could cut them and the herd right here.

That'd depend on the weather and the sheep. If the Basques were magicians at gathering the animals, and if the weather held, they could get past this nasty little rock fortress before Teton Jackson and his boys could occupy it.

The Basques were magicians. The weather broke bad. The wolves had been at the sheep.

Slocum caught the others easily. Horses broke a good sweat as the afternoon sun sank, and the shadows started to gather on the hilltops below them as they climbed. The trail got hard and rocky; it narrowed, so they rode single file and wrestled the buckboard through.

The first they saw of Murchison's sheep was the vultures. Everybody had half expected vultures, but nobody expected thousands of the big black birds.

Dark columns of vultures rising from the mountain meadow so green and so quiet after the bare slopes they had climbed all day. The buckboard steadied in the easy ground at the edge of the meadow.

They smelled dead sheep. The smell was sweet and clutched at your throat. Mary Anne Murchison pulled her neckerchief over her face, which helped some. The dead sheep were in all stages of decomposition. A few were broken down so far that only white clumps of wool on an indefinable something marked the carcass as a sheep. Some were fresher, with identifiable parts—head, front leg, a paunch, guts and all. Some of the corpses were bloated quite badly.

Arnaud's two guard dogs set up a frightful howling. Chained to the back of the buckboard, they barked and lunged so hard Smitty feared an upset.

Everybody wore a mask of indifference. What could panic or sadness do to make this better?

Murchison snarled that "Somebody should control those damn dogs or turn 'em loose. There's plenty critters in these woods that need killing."

Arnaud dismounted and took the near dog by its ruff and lifted it quite off the ground. The dog's toothy muzzle was a foot from his face. He shook the dog and spoke to it in the language of his people. He repeated the process with the second dog, and they both calmed some.

"The sheep are scattered," Arnaud said to Slocum. The two white dogs roved ahead of his horse, now obedient to his command. "The wolves have them trapped in this valley. It is good it is not spring, when wolves travel to find food for their cubs. It's not more than one pack eating the sheep."

They passed out of the woods into a open meadow—tufts of yellow-green grass grazed short. They found a band of woolies, eighty or a hundred strong. The sheep sentries posted on the outskirts whuffled their warning and stamped their hooves (so much like deer), and the flock bolted into the woods.

Arnaud stood in his stirrups. "Damn. I saw one of those wolf bastards. I'm not tall enough. Slocum, hand me my long gun." He climbed onto his saddle, fully erect, perfectly balanced. He calmed the horse with a murmur and extended his hand for his weapon.

Hell, Slocum couldn't see what he was aiming at. Just tall grass as far as he could see.

The gun spoke, the sharp crack of a light-caliber rifle. Arnaud yelled, "Two hundred yards from horseback! He is mine!"

When they rode over to the wolf's body, it was actually just over two hundred yards. Arnaud's bullet had taken it in the heart, and the animal managed only one bounding leap before it died in a heap.

When Arnaud started to skin the wolf, Mary Anne Murchison said they'd better start rounding up the sheep while there were still some left.

Arnaud straightened, his brass-hilted knife lying in his hand—a tool now, no weapon. "Miss Murchison, we always skin those who slay the sheep we guard," Arnaud explained slowly. "Always."

"If you don't stop messin' with that ugly dead thing, they'll kill what sheep we have left," she snapped, and put heels to her horse and stormed away.

"The *rubia* is a one, eh John?" Arnaud grinned. He made the long belly incision up to the V of the diaphragm. "These wolves in this valley . . ." he waved his bloody knife in a circle. He cut off the wolf's feet and slashed the white fur on the inside of the legs. Next, he peeled the hide down from the shoulders, leaving the animal a bloody-headed wolf from the head up and a bare piece of meat where the hide had been. "Here wolves are so fat from killing sheep they probably pant around all day in the heat of the sun." He kicked the carcass at his feet; sure enough, the beast wore a girdle of hard fat on its loin and hindquarters. Arnaud dipped his knife into the animal's stomach.

"He has eaten no mice. The wolves eat many mice, but not this wolf, no. It eats only livers and the blood of sheep. Look at this." Scuffing aside pieces of half-digested meat. "Those wolves are watching us at this very minute, John. They see us, wondering who we are and what we mean to do." He came out of his hunker, wiped the knife on the wolf hide, and rolled it up like a carpet under his arm. "So now they will see. They will see that we take the lives of their comrades, drain them, and carry them away. This is not a bad lesson for wolves to learn, yes?"

He opened the pelt. A wolf howled from back in the woods, and within seconds several other wolves joined in howling their grave song at the sky.

6

They made camp against the back of that little meadow. Smitty unpacked the buckboard, and the Basques put everybody except the boss to cutting poles. They started an enclosure and were still dragging poles to the site when the sun went down.

Smitty said, "Tomorrow this belly robber stays with his grub and don't work with you others. If you want me to put in a day's work I'll do it, but I won't cook your grub for you too."

Next morning Smitty was excused from the pole detail. Slocum and Mary Anne did most of the actual construction, lashing the poles together at the joints with strips of cloth, pegging skins and the remnants of Slocum's bloodstained shirt, torn in strips.

Each Basque rode out with two dogs—a herder and a guard dog. The guard dogs raced on ahead, searching out danger and allowing the herd dogs to sniff through the underbrush, scaring up small bands of sheep. If the guard dogs hadn't driven the wolves back, the wolves would have had the herding dogs for breakfast.

The top of that valley, where the sheep were boxed, was fairly dense underbrush and tight cedar forest. Except for the big meadow there wasn't much open land. In their panic the sheep had broken up into many bands, mostly small; the largest band was the one they'd spotted yesterday.

Slocum and Mary Anne hauled the poles into their zigzag, and flying fingers made the knots. If the sheep had been tame they wouldn't have needed this corral, but so it goes. They worked pretty well together. Mary Anne had a stubborn attention to her work that Slocum appreciated, and their minds worked alike. There weren't many times when she was trying to do one thing while he was trying to do another. Though she restricted her conversation to the job at hand, the cheerfulness in her voice was unmistakable. Unmistakable, too, the color mounting in her cheeks and the spring in her step.

They were fastening the last of their fence together when Arnaud came into the big meadow with the bunch they'd seen last night. The little herding dog raced around behind them full tilt. Arnaud told the dog where to go with cries and shouts that sounded like birds chirping. The dog reversed itself and shoved the sheep away from the sanctuary of the woods. The guard dog trotted beside Arnaud's horse, tongue lolling out, uncaring.

When the sheep were safely penned, John Slocum let out a whoop. "I make that sixty, seventy woolies! Just seven thousand some to go!"

Arnaud said, "Señor Slocum, we have a saying in my homeland: Do not count your lambs until they are sold. I have not seen very many living sheep."

A gust of cold wind. Slocum turned up his collar. Work had kept him warm, but it was clouding over, big blackheads piling up in the south and hurrying right along between the mountains. Another gust of wind.

Slocum said, "Oh shit!"

"I hope Smitty is keeping Father warm," Mary Anne said, turning her cheek from the weather.

"Smitty'll hold up his end," Slocum said. "I dunno what kind of weather this is—whether rain, sleet, or snow—but we can take it as a warning to get this job behind us."

When the sheet of icy, drizzling rain walked across the big meadow, it smashed the grass flat. The sheep they'd captured huddled together like mighty unhappy white mushrooms against the green grass.

Smitty laid a tarp under the buckboard and got the reluctant Murchison to crawl under it. He'd been sitting up on the seat, happy as could be, just watching his sheep graze and that miserable billowing sheet of water came across the meadow like the trumpets of the Lord.

Grumbling, he let Smitty help him to shelter. The wagon bed over his head made an imperfect roof, but Smitty strung other tarps to make a fairly cozy little cave where Murchison could watch them working when the sheets of rain cleared enough so he could see.

Smitty wore his long oilskin slicker, and his big hat kept the rain off his head, but nobody could move around in that rain very long without getting soaked. Smitty gathered dry firewood and strung another of his precious tarps so the cookfire would continue to burn. He stored the firewood at Murchison's feet.

Sabrina brought in a dozen sheep. Her herding dog looked like a drowned water rat, its long hair dangling from its body. It had to work much harder in the rain, because the sheep were miserable and unwilling to move.

When Sabrina had her bunch safely corraled she came to the cookfire. Smitty lifted the cover on a steaming pot of fatback and beans. He had a metal box that kept his biscuits dry, and the coffee that burbled in the pot smelled—and was—delicious. Sabrina scooted under the wagon and ate the good hot food and watched her saddle turn black and slippery with water.

The food warmed her gut, and the coffee warmed her hands. Murchison asked her how many sheep she'd seen.

"Señor, I do not know. In that short brush, with the rain in your face and the low branches picking at your clothes, it is fortunate we have the dogs or we would be unable to gather a single sheep."

Twenty minutes later she was back in the woods, the dogs coursing ahead of her.

Slocum and Mary Anne rushed into the meadow, hot on the heels of a tiny band. After busting through the woods for what seemed like forever, they collected four miserable sheep for their efforts. Angrily they penned them.

A polite Smitty advised, "You can't work those critters like they was cows. I told Renfrew that, and now I'm tellin' you."

Slocum practically bit his head off. Hollered for his grub like he expected Smitty to be empty-handed. Truth was, John Slocum had eaten the dust of many a cow, but the closest he'd ever been to sheep was at the livestock market back home in Georgia. He didn't

know them like he did cows, and he sure as hell
didn't like them. He said so.

Mary Anne, who was just as wet and miserable,
agreed with him completely. After they ate they felt
better, despite Murchison's hectoring. He wanted to
see more sheep out in the corral, because that's what
they'd come for—not to fight all the rough customers
in the territory. "Leave Teton Jackson be," he
smoothly advised. "Just get back out there and col-
lect those Muleshoe woolies." He grimaced. The
grimace was meant to be a smile. "Don't go back in
the woods just to fool around." He waggled one gray
finger at them. "I know you two been courtin'," he
said.

"There's no fool like an old fool," Slocum said.

For all their complaints, they didn't stay in the
relative comfort of the buckboard any longer than
Sabrina had. It wasn't fun getting back in the saddle,
but they managed it.

The downpour varied between rain and frozen sleet.
One was no better than the other. Every time they'd
come on the sheep—and there were a few out there—
Slocum would try to get around them and start like
he did calves. He soon learned to go wider and
slower. Slocum and Mary Anne brought in groups of
three and four at a time. Sabrina's bunches were
much bigger—thirty or forty, and one batch of over
fifty.

When it started darkening, Smitty laced their coffee with whiskey.

Arnaud came in with the last possible light, and
they could hear him long before they got a glimpse of
him—the noise of a large flock of sheep, baaing,

calling, marching under command. They came into the meadow like a sea of yellow-white foam. Arnaud's dog hurried them into the curve toward the gate, and Sabrina took her dog out to help.

When they closed the gate of their makeshift corral, the light was gone.

Only the little cave was dry. The buckboard had a long enough bed so they could just fit under the shelter if they all faced the same way. Murchison lay dead center before the fire. He was full of questions.

"Five hundred, total," Arnaud said. "I gathered the bands together before I brought them in. There are more sheep out there."

A wolf howled. One of the guard dogs set up barking. Both guard dogs were with the flock tonight, unchained, lying right beside their charges. The herding dogs had found a dry corner under the buckboard.

They finished eating and were asleep almost before they handed their plates back to Smitty. He stayed awake, listening to the wolves out in the rain and wondering how soon he and Red Smart would come face to face. He owed him for the Wolf Kid. What had Slocum said? Sunday morning. Three more days.

In the morning Murchison was no better and no worse. He ate pretty good, but he coughed quite a bit, because the rain was blowing under the lip of the buckboard in the gray light. He was too miserable to care about his sheep, and his shepherds were too miserable to assure him.

The rain that had fallen during the night clung to the trees, sheathing the wood with ice—glistening coverlets over every cedar branch and every rock beside the trail. The corral poles glistened like railroad rails on a hot day. They walked their horses where they could, because the footing was so bad. They traveled in two teams of two, following the herding dogs, which were the only animals in this foul weather who could do much good.

During the blind night the guard dogs had taken a wolf that came in to test the flock's defenses. Like most wolves, this pilgrim had no particular fear of dogs. Those he couldn't outfight he could outrun. Usually.

In the morning light the shepherds rode past the corpse of the pilgrim, throat torn out.

"Ain't you gonna skin him?" Slocum asked.

"I only skin the ones I kill. If this ice turns to snow, we shall play hell getting down to the lowlands, amigo."

By the end of that day they had rounded up a thousand sheep and returned them to the corral. The rain didn't let up, but it didn't turn to snow either. Nobody was dry or cheerful, but none of the horses fell badly on the bad footing. The guard dogs trapped another wolf. He got away but left a few parts of himself dangling from the enormous jaws of the big white dogs.

The next day they gathered another thousand. They'd learned how to work together, moving slowly and deliberately. The little dogs did most of the work; the riders just helped them and made their work easier. Come lunchtime, the dogs dropped off for twenty minutes sleep, and at night they slept a few minutes after they ate their dinner. They lost weight but not heart.

Saturday they made the biggest gather of all. They located a large bunch by the far end of the valley and spent hours pushing them along. They had too many sheep now for their makeshift corral but had no time to rebuild it. They lay down Saturday night, exhausted to the bone—man, woman, and horse, dog and sheep.

And it was starting to snow.

7

The snow came swirling down, big fat flakes that served notice of winter's intention to reclaim this country for its own. The sun shone behind the snow the way it will sometimes, but it never got strong enough to melt the flakes that began to haze the trees, the rocks, the sheep's backs.

Four out of eight. By quick work they'd saved half the animals. Though there were probably another couple of hundred animals hiding in the bush, they'd left them for the wolves.

In the morning they stepped into a half inch of snow—grumpy, stiff, and battered. The guard dogs had had a quiet night guarding the augmented flock; the wolves had learned their lesson. When Smitty started rattling around, two white-covered shapes detached themselves from the mounded white sheep and came wagging in for a handout. The old cook slipped them some meat scraps and shooed them back to work.

Slocum was the next to rise. He took his coffee with no sugar or cream or thanks. He sipped the steaming stuff while he examined the world.

Before everybody else had finished breakfast, Slocum was out graining the horses. The oats they carried would have to do them for rations now. Sheep could paw the snow away to get at the dead grasses underneath.

Quick as that they were packed up and on the move. Arnaud and the herding dogs brought up the rear, then Murchison and the women in the buckboard, Smitty out front on the big flock with Slocum.

The guard dogs trotted alongside the buckboard like that's where they belonged.

Smitty had been pleased when Slocum asked him to ride point, but when thoughts of Teton Jackson started crowding in, he had to stiffen his resolve and bear down. Slocum carried his rifle across his saddlebow and paid no attention to the flock they'd just spent so much time and effort gathering. His attention was fixed on the trail ahead. He rode easy, but he rode wary, too. His eyes scanned from side to side in that careful constant movement that'll detect the tiniest motion.

Sometime this morning, Teton Jackson would hit this trail—if he had ridden like a bat out of hell. Slocum had no reason to suppose he wouldn't have.

No telling how many men with him. Probably most of the riders that had accompanied his drive into Wyoming would come back—those that weren't anxious to head south for the winter. Say half of them. That'd be eight men, from the tracks they'd left beside the marks of their stolen herd. Then there'd be the messengers from Jackson's roadhouse. Probably four or five more. In any fight you always kill somebody's pal or father or brother, and there's always several in the family anxious to take revenge. Figure one man for every man they'd dropped back at the roadhouse. Say eight again. Maybe nine.

Expect Teton Jackson with near twenty men sometime today. That's what they rode toward and why Slocum's eyes never stopped moving. They wouldn't have much chance in a stand-up fight against numbers like those. Sometimes one man will be the equal of three or four in a fight, but no man can consistently take on that kind of odds and live.

And Teton's men wouldn't be babes in the woods. They'd be hardcases, every one, quick to shoot and quicker to backshoot.

The sheep were stepping along briskly enough at a good steady walk. Already Arnaud and his dogs had them trail-broke. Smitty turned around in the saddle and shook his head. That was the difference, he thought, between knowing and not knowing.

Riding on either side of the ailing Murchison, the two women endured every bump and jostle of the buckboard same as he did. Sabrina had her shotgun under her lap robe, and the two dogs jogging alongside would kill anything she told them to. She was unhappy because she wanted to be riding with Arnaud doing real work, not being jarred and bumped in this uncomfortable buckboard guarding the stupid *rubia* and her garrulous father.

Murchison was full of advice and meant to unburden himself: "Now you feed these ewes about five pounds of hay every day and plenty of water and come March you'll have enough lambs to replace most of your loss. There's hay for the whole flock at the home place and then some. If weather gets bad the cowmen will be screaming for hay same as always. Get a good price for it, buy into their herds if you can, because in another couple years I'm gonna get back into cattle. . . . *You* can get back into cattle when there's a good shortage and the price is on the climb. Now, about the watering . . ."

He went on like that for an hour, filling Mary Anne's ears with more information than she could possibly take in. Mary Anne had the reins. Naught to do but listen as the rancher poured out his life. He spoke about the wife he'd loved, the mother his daughter had scarcely known. He told her how he'd felt when she left this world, victim of a cholera epidemic that had ravaged the territory just fifteen years ago, killing Indians and settlers alike.

"I might have been different had she lived," he said. "I guess when she went away I figured that I had to be hard to survive, so I got hard and stayed that way. That was always a tendency I had—daughter, you have it too—and it's something I've learned to regret. Everybody takes the same blows during their life, and nobody is ever hard enough to take them."

Mary Anne's ears perked up when he mentioned her, but when he continued philosophizing, she shut down again. She drove on, attentive to the voice inside her—her list of complaints. Though she'd tolerate much to recover the wealth the flock represented, she cursed every dirty weary moment of it.

The new snow glistened on the trail ahead and on the branches of the trees. Snow as soft as moth wings. Her brain told her it was cold and thus ugly. Even her father's chatter upset her. Caring for the old man, she'd come to honestly hate him. He was such a burden. He could hardly walk unaided now, and she'd had to assist him in almost everything. Smitty did the supporting when the old man had to answer a call of nature; his daughter was far too delicate for that task.

Though she knew it was wicked of her to wish it, she'd often wished—well, she hadn't wished him dead; she was no monster, after all. But she had wished things finished, which was another word altogether.

"When I first came into this country," the old man blathered on, "it was so goddamn beautiful it took your breath away. There was as much land then as a man could take and hold with his own strength. Hold it against bad weather and bad markets, Indians, rustlers, and plain old bad luck. Lord, there's been enough of bad luck in my life. Hell, if you put a stone over me, daughter, just put my name on it and my dates. 'J.D. Murchison: Boss of Bad Luck.' That'd be about right. That'd suit me."

"Daddy, don't worry," she said mechanically. "You'll be fine once we get down to the ranch and you start to get your strength back. Smitty'll cook up that broth that does you so much good, and Renfrew'll work the sheep, and Slocum can help him out, and"— with a glance at the dark-haired woman—"we can be among our own kind again."

Sabrina shot her a dagger glance. The *rubia* was so very very stupid. The fierce Basque woman liked Murchison all right, and she was the one listening to the old man's stories. But the daughter was not the same stock.

The woolies came on behind at a regular pace. Normally Arnaud would have pressed them slower first day on the trail, but not this morning; he couldn't.

The trail narrowed, and the column thinned out and got very much longer. Slocum and Smitty stayed a couple of hundred yards ahead of the buckboard.

If Teton Jackson met them on this part of the trail, the men on point would be dead as hell with no way to retreat through the packed sheep behind them.

The sheep pushed along nose to tail, six wide, a solid block of patiently plodding animals. One dog worked behind and the other stayed on the slope above, so none would be tempted to climb away from the press.

John Slocum couldn't get more careful. A man could only get so careful before the measures he took for his safety confused things.

Ahead, like a rooster spur, he saw that fort of rock he'd explored on the way up. If Teton Jackson and his bunch had got there yet, that's where they'd be.

His eyes flicked over the rock escarpments and the cedar fringe. He spotted a couple of brown wrens in the cedar bush pecking for the juniper berries that fruited this time of year, but he didn't see any men. The rock spur that so dominated the countryside had the feel of desertion, and Slocum knew to credit his instincts.

From a thousand yards, the rocky spur looked formidable. At five hundred yards it seemed impossible: two hundred feet of weathered rock. The base was a talus mound, and the almost sheer walls climbed out of the broken rock like the stump of a tree.

John Slocum knew what he had to do but was reluctant. He eyeballed the long hogback, the empty trail where Jackson and his riders must certainly come, riding like the hounds of hell after the men who'd stung their pride and their honor.

Slocum drew rein at the fork. No sign from the Wyoming branch of the trail. No footprints in the uniform light covering of snow.

Snow covered the goods and tarps in the buckboard. There was snow on the brim of J.D. Murchison's hat, and cold vapor formed at his nose. His nose was red, but the hands that gripped the buckboard seat looked pretty healthy.

Slocum touched his hat brim to the ladies. "How you feelin' Mr. Murchison?" That "mister" should have tipped Murchison that something was up, but he didn't notice the modest little show of respect. "I'd like to talk to you."

His hat tilted back and his eyes narrowed. "Speak up then, boy. No reason to be shy."

"I'll talk to you alone."

"Nothing I'll say my daughter can't hear. I'm training her for the management of Muleshoe, and she's got to know all the details."

"Training time's done, Mr. Murchison."

"Oh." His face got all quiet and thoughtful, and then he told his daughter she should go on down the trail a bit and watch for Teton Jackson. Sabrina was glad to mount her horse and take the point as the sheep spilled around the turn and started toward the lower valley.

"I'll just move this buggy over here where we can talk. Damn woolies make such a racket I can't hear myself think."

When they were free of the herd, John Slocum took time to roll himself a quirly. He said, "I wish I had a Havana, but I'm all out."

"Build me a smoke, then," J.D. replied. "Something's always better than nothing."

"I'm sorry you feel that way," Slocum said, but built the rancher a cigarette and tossed it over. The man's lined face in the flare of the match.

"Sure is fine country," Slocum said.

"You bet it is. God's country."

"If it was me dyin', I'd hate to leave it."

"I wish it was you instead of me."

Slocum grinned at the sick man, and Murchison found strength for a grin in return. "If Teton Jackson comes up that trail"—Slocum pointed it out—"he'll be behind us. He's likely to have a few *compañeros*, and I understand they're to be feared. Arnaud and me are men to be feared too, but there's only two of us. The others can handle the flock while we fight, but once we fall the flock'll have no protection, and I guess the women won't have any protection either. I'll tell Sabrina to kill Mary Anne if she's in danger of falling into Jackson's hands alive. Those big white dogs hold the wolves back, but I expect some of them are out there now, shadowing the flock. There's a winter's feeding out here for wolves, and I expect they'll keep it in mind. If Jackson doesn't kill the dogs, too, they'll protect the flock, but the wolves will have them before ice-out in the spring."

Murchison's gaze was as dispassionate as Slocum's own. "You called me over to tell me this? That all the work and money and effort is for naught? You called me out to tell me we'll all die and lose the animals, too?"

"That's the way I see it." Slocum shrugged. " 'Course we could abandon the sheep and just run like hell."

J.D. Murchison tried to stand up, and he managed it with one hand on the buckboard rail for balance. "Like hell we will," he said.

"Maybe we can make it. It's no more than four hours down that trail until it broadens, and we'd have more room to maneuver. We'll have no chance if he catches up with us where we can't fight."

"I suppose you got something in mind."

Slocum was blunt. "You can buy us the time. If you're willing to die."

Explosive bark of laughter. "Willing or unwilling. I ain't got very much choice in that matter."

John Slocum turned to point. "A man on top of that rock there, he could hold this junction for a fair time."

Innocently, Murchison said, "Do tell."

"Sure. One man with a rifle—he'd have to be a marksman, mind you—he could tear a chunk off anybody wanting to pass."

"Do tell. You wouldn't have no whiskey in that saddlebag of yours?"

"I might." He pulled the cork and gave it to the old rancher for the first swallow. Murchison was as delighted as a kid. It was a great boy's game they

were playing. A game that would leave him dead
before noon. Murchison took a deep swallow of that
cheap medicinal whiskey, and it tasted like ambrosia
to him. Like life itself.

Not many can choose to go out and have it serve
some purpose.

"I am a fair hand with a Henry .44," Murchison
admitted modestly.

"You need cartridges. I wouldn't be surprised to
see Jackson riding with twenty men. That sort always
likes to travel in mobs. But don't mistake them. Give
them no quarter, because they won't give you none."

Murchison snorted. "Boy, you tryin' to teach your
granny how to suck eggs?"

So. Okay. Slocum nodded. He stuck out his hand.
"We ain't been pals, Murchison, but I'm proud to
have known you."

The old man straightened up and seemed to glow
with energy. "Then you can leave me that bottle,"
he said.

"Uh-huh. We'll leave you plenty of comforts.
You won't lack a thing up there."

"Including targets." The old man chuckled.

While Slocum waited for Arnaud, Murchison beckoned his daughter to his side. He said, "Tell the truth
now, daughter, do we really care so very much for
one another?"

Honestly startled her. Mary Anne was accustomed
to a screen of good manners and blushed furiously.
"Daddy, you know we do. Why, we're all the family
we've got. We—"

"Honey, don't throw bullshit at the bull who made

it. We ain't never been particular close. Neither of us really had the time, I reckon, but I seen closer families than you and me have been.''

She met his eyes unflinchingly. "I reckon that's true," she said, because it was.

"Good." He noted his satisfaction. "There's one thing we always cared about, and that's Muleshoe. I expect we both rightly love that ranch.''

She thought that was true. She knew it was true in her heart. "I can't imagine living without Muleshoe," she said. For her the world ended at Muleshoe's property line.

Murchison told her about Slocum's fears. He described the death of the party and the loss of Muleshoe's flock. "I aim to get up there on that rock top and hold them until you get the flock clear.''

She shaded her eyes. The rock pile looked like a haystack dusted with snow. It looked cold. "You'll need a blanket," she said.

"Uh-huh." He scoured his daughter's face for any sign kinder than honesty but saw none. She was every bit as hard as he was. He waited, giving her a chance to say more, but apparently her observation about the blanket had exhausted her emotional store. "I ain't gonna climb back down off that rock," he finally said.

She just looked at him. Surely that was obvious.

His smile had worn soft regret. "It would have been better if your mother had lived," he said. "She would have taught us both a few tricks.''

No comment. His daughter was as rigid as a stick. He wanted to embrace her but satisfied himself with an awkward pat on her shoulders. "You'll take care of Muleshoe," he said.

"I will," she said.

"Marry John Slocum," he said.

She showed the first faint signs of doubt. Her eyes softened. "I don't believe . . ."

He didn't give her any more mercy than she'd shown. He was on her that fast. "You'll need a man to hold Muleshoe."

"I am not exactly unattractive."

"I ain't blind." Testily. "Now listen to me when I give you good advice."

She set her jaw stubbornly.

"Mistake you made was letting him have you too soon, daughter. If you'd kept it out in front of him like a carrot before a donkey, you'd surely have snared that man, and he'd help you hold Muleshoe against all comers." He laughed. "Unless John Slocum found you more useful on a rock with a rifle in your hand. You'll have to watch that tendency in him, Mary Anne. He's the last one on the raft when the ship goes down, that one."

"I will do what I must. Father, I must remind you that you cannot control Muleshoe from . . . where you're going."

Though she'd stumbled, she'd managed to tell him to mind his own business, sharp as can be. Had to admire a woman like that. Maybe she wouldn't need a man to hold Muleshoe.

Arnaud's two dogs pushed the last of the sheep around the bend. Slocum flagged Arnaud. The two men put their heads together, and both Murchisons saw him point at the rock. The Murchisons watched because they couldn't think of anything more to say to each other. They never had been too free with words, and the present occasion couldn't create sound in a space that had been too long silent.

The two men rode closer to the rock, and Arnaud did his trick again—climbed right up on the saddle so he could see better.

Mary Anne thought it looked like a circus trick. She found it tasteless.

Once again Slocum tipped his hat to Mary Anne. "Mr. Murchison, there's a good game trail up that side of the rock. I don't think you're in any condition to climb it unaided. Maybe there's an easier pitch around the far side, but if there isn't we'll waste time looking. Jackson's overdue now. Arnaud'll clamber on up. Between his rope and me, we'll get you up there in one piece."

Murchison opened his mouth but closed it again.

"Good-bye," his daughter said.

"Good-bye." His voice cracked, and his farewell came out a croak. Carefully he slid to the ground, where Slocum took his arm.

Arnaud hurried on ahead with the gear Murchison would need. The old man and Slocum walked to the start of the game trail, Murchison almost walking by himself. He never looked back. He'd said what good-byes he meant to.

With the help of the rope Arnaud dropped, the climb wasn't so bad. Murchison kept the loop under his armpits, and anytime he started to feel dizzy or sick he let the rope take his weight. The game trail

was no more than that—scarcely two feet wide—and
Slocum couldn't help much behind him.

The top of the rock slab was shaped like a rough
triangle with the long point aiming out over the
countryside where Jackson must come from. The tip
commanded a sheer precipice, directly above the trail
junction.

"You can see a long way up here. Hell, I believe
those mountains must be in Wyoming."

"You gonna let me down or you gonna rubber-
neck?" Murchison demanded. He settled himself on
the wool blanket Arnaud had laid out right at the tip.
It felt good to sit. The climb had cost him something,
and he had to catch his breath.

"I'm leavin' you my repeating rifle," Slocum said.
"This Henry is sighted in perfect for two hundred
yards. Hold six inches high for three hundred. Don't
do any shooting over that range."

"You gonna be up here with me?" Murchison
demanded.

"I'm riding with the flock," Slocum said. "I told
you that."

"Fine. Then don't go giving me advice. Jesus
Christ, I go all through my whole damn life, not
needin' no advice or instructions, and I done pretty
good, too, by God. So I get to the last few hours and
every damn fool around starts telling me how to
spend my time. Now ain't that peculiar." He drawled
the word "peculiar," tasting every syllable.

"I suppose so. You got two cartons of ammunition—that's a hundred bullets in all."

"Give me another box, boy. Don't you expect me
to do any good at all?"

"Sure." Slocum left another fifty rounds. "Smitty sent this." Inside a cotton muslin sack was the butt of the ham they'd been nibbling. "It'll keep pretty good." Slocum unslung his canteen and laid it beside the ham.

Arnaud said something in Basque tongue and translated. "Go with God, señor. We will bring your flock back to the ranch."

"If we'd had a few like you, we wouldn't have lost it in the first place. You tell Mary Anne that you got a job at Muleshoe whenever you want. You're a top hand." The boss waved, motioning the help away, imperious to the end.

And Slocum laid his Bull Durham on the old man's blanket. He left. They had nothing more to say to each other.

Murchison heard Slocum's boots on the trail, and finally he heard Arnaud's call: "Adios, señor." Their horses started down the trail. Good. He was alone.

From these heights the gentle rolling hills glowed with snowfall. He hoped it didn't get to snowing hard or he wouldn't see them coming. The brush stuck out like pepper flakes. The wind tossed snow spume on distant ridge tops, faint and ethereal.

He jacked the lever partway open, noting that Slocum had left one up the spout. He set the stock into his shoulder and watched the landscape through the sights. He grunted and rolled his extra blanket under his arm for a rest. Man with a good rest always got off a better shot. He propped the Henry on his makeshift pad and opened the boxes of shells, examining them one at a time, looking for defects—an oddly shaped primer or marred wax on the tips. The suspicious rounds, fourteen in all, he set aside for last, after the others were gone. There weren't as many defects as there would have been ten years earlier. Makers had learned to make ammunition that was almost perfectly reliable.

He wished he had another couple of boxes to examine but he didn't. The snow drifted down gently on his sheepskin, the first coat of thick paint that'd lock up the country. But he wasn't noticing the snow. He began to lose the feeling in his legs but didn't care very much. He figured his body would withdraw into the citadel to give him vision and strength.

What a joke! What a funny damn way to die!

He wondered if he'd see his wife. He wondered how he'd explain what he'd done with his life. Probably he wouldn't see her in the afterlife. Of the two possible destinations, he was sure they were ticketed differently.

The snow came down, implacable, and melted on the back of his hand. It was wet and raw and gray. The moons in his fingernails were vivid. Murchison had been born in Iowa. He wondered if the winters were any less rough in Iowa. He'd been gone so long that he couldn't easily remember. He'd lost those days of his youth, even to his memory. He hadn't thought it would come to that. He focused behind his eyes and tried to conjure up his dead wife's face. The only face he could call to mind was the daguerreotype he kept on his dresser back at Muleshoe. Used to be he could recall dozens of views of his wife: a picture of her smiling as she gathered up spring daisies, her skirt rucked up as a basket; a picture of her riding beside him that day they rode down to the springs for an outing. Her face is turned to his . . .

Forget it. Man's got more important things to think about than the dead. Unless he's about to get in that condition himself. Then there doesn't seem to be that much difference between the here and the gone.

Murchison took the tiniest taste of whiskey. Just wet his lips. No sense letting the whiskey fumes go to his head. He roved his gaze over the distant slopes before he rolled himself a quirly. He lit a lucifer and took a puff and got some sulfur from the match and stubbed it out, thinking that probably it was going to be his last cigarette, and it was funny—he didn't even want it. Same with the whiskey. Now that he could have what he wanted, he didn't want it anymore.

The trail rose out of Wyoming on fat hills that rolled like a woman's hips. It was a good fast trail— which was why Teton Jackson preferred it for his stolen cows—and except where the snow had melted and made it wet, Jackson's bunch had made pretty good time. Though the ground wasn't frozen solid, it was hard enough for horse's hooves.

They came across the horizon like hurrying dots, just cleared the top of one ridge and dipped out of sight behind the second one.

Murchison's heart skipped a beat. "Goddamn it," he growled. "Now you don't quit on me now. We got a bit of hard work to do."

Up over a second ridge and stayed visible for a longer time than before. Enough for Murchison to count them. Twenty-three riders, riding hard. Maybe a mile and a half but coming on in a hurry.

Murchison was grinning like a fool, like a kid.

The gray sky was lowering now, and far behind the racing riders, the mountains of Wyoming were dipping behind veils of weather. A clump of snow hung from the very brim of J.D.'s Stetson. The trail passed so close under his gun he could damn near spit onto the junction. That's how close they'd have to come.

He wondered how many of these men he knew. There weren't so many white men in this part of the country. Probably some of Jackson's gang were native to Wyoming. He couldn't say. Those hombres knew how to ride! Murchison had always loved horse-flesh, and the animals racing toward him ran like prime specimens, the gait just short of a full gallop, which a good horse could maintain all day.

They'd be in long range in another few seconds. He slid the Henry forward and pressed his cheek against the stock. The stock was cold and wet. It'd get warm soon enough. The riders were dots that danced on the end of his sight, above the sight blade, below it. That must be Jackson himself, the big gent in the middle. No other kind of fool wears that many furs. Why, he's dressed like a mountain man. A good shot past his horse's neck would take him somewhere in the middle, right in the guts. Move the sight blade over a hair and the bullet might tick the liver.

J.D. Murchison hoped Teton Jackson would scream. Four hundred yards. His thumb drew the hammer back and he settled into the position, took a good breath, and damned if it didn't seem like that front V-sight magnified everything, because he could see old Teton Jackson just fine, and that pale fellow on his right, that must be Red Smart. God, what an ugly son.

They rode silently, with the deadly silence of coursing hounds. Sometimes Teton Jackson in front of the gang, sometimes, like now, the man they called Butch. Butch had plenty of brains, and he'd been the one who'd figured out about the good trail to Wyoming and keeping the sheep off it. It'd been him who reacted first and fastest to the alarm from the roadhouse.

Butch had said, "It's them or us," which was about the way it was.

The bullet killed him on the spot. He took the slug meant for his boss.

"Damn," Murchison cursed, levering another. His next slug killed Teton Jackson's horse. Teton Jackson lit running and though Murchison would have sworn there wasn't a rock on that slope big enough to hide behind, he found one.

The riders came on and he levered twice more, firing carefully, and he dropped a pair for his trouble.

Jackson's bunch was firing back, answering his invitation, but a sixgun isn't that much use from the back of a racing horse, and none of their slugs came close. He got him another one, just put a pill right in the rider's head and the man clapped hands over his wound and rolled right back off his saddle.

Murchison laughed. It was like a pigeon shoot, when the big flocks of passenger pigeons darken the sky. A man can't help killing one, no matter where he points his rifle.

He killed another man. It was easy.

The riders were hollering now, and some of them were riding Indian-style, slid way over on their horses. All that was visible was one hand on the horse's mane and the foot thrown over the animal's rump. By God, if he was to hold just right . . . The Henry bucked and spat its hundred-grain bullet across intervening space to smash a man's foot. He drops from his horse, under the hooves, and Murchison can't see him anymore.

"Hah!" he yells. Red Smart is out in front now. Once they reach the junction, they can find some cover for sure.

The Henry clicks empty. Oh, don't his fingers work to stuff more shells into the rifle's gut! He skids them through the loading gate one after another. He's shaking, and only the rifle at his shoulder can stop the shakes.

Oh Jesus, they're almost past, and their bullets are buzzing now, and he doesn't give a good goddamn and kills another man. Smart's found cover. Others lay their horses down—the cavalryman's trick—for a ready-made fort.

He fires into the smoke and hears a horse scream. A slug screes off the rock. Another whips his coat sleeve. He wounds, wounds again. He wounds a horse who goes cat-jumping off the edge of the ridge, making tremendous twenty-foot jumps.

The men below couldn't get a shot unless he stuck his head out, which he wasn't doing. They could pepper the rock and did. Red Smart worked his way around the rock, below the unknown rifleman's circle of vision, and a couple of other boys came around on the far side. Teton Jackson lay very small behind his insufficient cover boulder and yelled for a truce.

After a bit, his bunch stopped firing. "Hey! You on the rock. You! What the hell you want?"

The voice that sang from above them was faint, clear, almost feminine. "J.D. Murchison. You interfered with my livestock." Jackson's face was pressed against the cold ground. A bullet from Murchison nearly took his eyelashes off and filled his mouth with sputter. "Goddamn. Goddamn. Goddamn you, Murchison! You got no call to do this!"

Jackson's voice was a howl. It sounded much like a wolf howl. J.D. Murchison noted the resemblance and tried another shot.

A bullet cut through Murchison's hat, just kind of puffing the hat higher without dislodging it. He tugged it back in place and tried two quick ones at the near riders. No dice. He killed the horses the men had laid down before them hoping the animal's death agonies would open a clean shot.

Mulrchison fired again and again, but never with the same deadly efficiency. One shot after another and no more hits.

Teton Jackson broke from cover and made a long looping dive into a gully and Murchison missed him clean.

Murchison felt like his blood was retreating toward the center of his body. He wondered what time it was. The sun was behind the swirling snow. His shoulder ached where the recoil of so many shots had pounded it. His right eye burned from the powder blown black from the Henry's receiver. His blanket was covered with brilliant gold cartridge cases. He wondered how he had never noticed before how pretty they were. . . .

When Red Smart finally climbed Murchison's fort, he found a dead man without a bullet hole in him. The dead man had a couple of spent cases in his right hand. He was smiling, which enraged Red Smart so much he kicked the unresisting body to the edge of the precipice and over.

8

They had pushed the sheep two hours before they heard the shots. At this distance, farther down the mountain, the popping sounded more like distant hammering than a fight.

Mary Anne Murchison shed tears. Sabrina dismounted to walk beside the buckboard and offer what consolation she could. "Your father, he is a brave man."

"He's a Murchison." The pride smashing through the tears.

Sabrina couldn't think of anything to add to that. At that distance rifles and pistols sound pretty much the same, and there's no distinction between friends and foes.

The snow was melting at the lower elevation, and sixteen thousand sharp little hooves can make a mess out of the hardest trail. Pools appeared behind rock coffer dams and banks disappeared into soft quavering mounds of wet earth.

At the narrowest places, the buckboard's off wheels rolled along a bank with a two-hundred-foot scree slope yawning below. Slocum dismounted and clambered up the slope, leading his surefooted animal. He checked through the jumble of rock slabs and boulders.

A couple of years ago this slope had felt the shock of an avalanche. Great trees were uprooted, and the rock was sheered off by the snowfield far above them. One slab the size of a railroad car had uprooted, flopped over, slid its snout into the trail, and gouged it out of existence.

The detour dipped below the nose of that huge slab of slippery rock. It was so steep that the horses set their heels against the downhill pull, and Mary Anne hauled hard on the wooden handle of the wheel brake. The slippery trail didn't give much purchase, and Mary Anne was popping her brake and catching it again because either free-wheeling or wheel-locked would spell a slide into her horse's hocks, and once the horses lost their balance, well, it surely was a long way to fall.

The shots stopped.

Mary Anne held that squeeling protesting brake hard against the inner hub of the wheels. It screamed and screamed.

He was dead.

The buckboard passed under the snout of the boulder, and once Mary Anne was past the rock's irregular face the trail climbed back to the level where it had been until it had been so rudely interrupted.

The snow in Mary Anne Murchison's face made tracks as it melted into tears.

Smitty rode point. Arnaud and his dogs kept the sheep moving at a pretty good clip. When John Slocum came down off his slope, Sabrina came up beside him. His horse was wet with sweat.

"The shooting, señor, it has stopped."

"Yeah."

"They will be coming after us now."

"I expect they will. This trail is pretty hard to miss."

"Mr. Murchison, he is dead?"

"Likely he's found the gate to shadowland."

"Shadowland?"

"That's what the Sioux call it—the plains where souls wander after their death, fighting old enemies and helped by their old allies. He said he liked the notion."

"You are not a Christian, señor?"

"Don't rightly know what I am. I expect Murchison died happy."

"And you, Mr. Slocum. Will you die happy? I have observed you, señor, these days on the trail, and it has made me wonder. You are a man of very great qualities, señor. I wonder why you do the work you do."

Slocum gave her a look. That was a hell of a question, and he wasn't sure she had a right to ask it. He figured it was two or three in the afternoon. It'd get dark soon after five, and then it would be stalemate. The sheep would have to stop, and unless the sky cleared for a big moon, Teton Jackson's men would stop too. Murchison had bought them the time to get off the narrow part of the trail, but they'd have fighting tomorrow.

"Señor, you do not answer me."

"Generally I don't answer insults with words, ma'am." He touched the brim of his hat.

"I didn't mean it as an insult, Mr. Slocum."

"Uh-huh." He looked at the woman's hawklike profile, her strong horseman's seat. Her jacket couldn't quite hide her sharp breasts.

"We save money, Arnaud and I. Soon we will have enough for our own flock. One day we will buy land, and then we will be ranchers like Mr. Murchison. Do you not believe me, Mr. Slocum?"

"Sure. You two ought to do fine. Unless you both die out here from Teton Jackson's bullets."

She sat up straighter. "I am not afraid. Arnaud has never found a man he feared."

"Yep." He rode along loosely. He shielded his papers and rolled a quirly. He exhaled a thin stream of smoke.

"Why do you say nothing, Slocum? You answer few of my questions."

"Some questions don't need answering, Sabrina."

"Now you taunt me, señor."

"I think highly of you and your brother. I've never seen anybody like you two for running a flock of sheep. I am proud to know the both of you, but I wouldn't want you as friends."

Well, that sat her up straight. "Señor, that is a very strange attitude."

"Not so strange. I travel alone. Those who try to stay with me die, like as not. I'd rather steer clear. Sometimes I think I've got a mistaken way of doing things, but by now it's gotten to be a habit."

"I see." For a few minutes she was quiet. The slushy snow melted in the air in front of her face. The wind swirled wetness into her face. Slocum spat his ruined quirly beside the trail. The sheep marched forward, harried constantly by the dogs.

One, two more switchbacks and they'd be off the worst of the trail. There'd be bad patches farther on, but there'd be miles of open country, too.

"If it snows good tonight, we might slip them," Slocum noted.

"I see." She pursed her face. "Señor, have you ever been married?"

"No. A couple times I been close, but I never took the plunge."

"Will you marry, señor?"

"You know what I think, Sabrina? I think you got too many questions by a long sight and you keep a man from thinking about the job at hand—which is, in case you have forgotten, pulling through this afternoon and tonight and tomorrow with the sheep."

"Yes, señor. I do not ask about the obvious." She smiled at him like a pixie and clucked to her horse, and it moved on ahead.

The sheep turned onto the last switchback and Arnaud sent one of his herding dogs ahead to keep the flock from scattering in the woods. The dog hurtled full tilt down the slope, and Slocum wondered briefly if very many of the herding dogs died trying to do their job. Probably.

Smitty was at the buckboard, pulling dry provisions out of his trunks and cases. Cold beef on cold biscuits wasn't gourmet fare, but it'd keep them going. The flock spread out under the trees, grazing, and Arnaud had the oat bucket on his horse, getting food to him while he could.

Slocum dismounted and rubbed his hands together. Wet. Cold. If the temperature dropped a few degrees it'd be snow again. Snow would cover their tracks, but there was only one way out of these mountains.

"If there's another way down to Muleshoe, Smitty might know it," he counseled Arnaud.

Arnaud's sharp black eyes. "And you?"

"I figure Jackson and his boys are still coming on. I don't know how many, but they'll be after our scalps, and I guess they'll have enough light to finish it. I might hold them up until dark."

"I see."

"If I get lost up there and don't find my way back, you honcho the outfit."

"Surely. I suppose this is a good time to die as any. I wish my sister weren't with us."

"Yeah. This ain't quite the place."

"It's cold."

"It is."

"Take one of the guard dogs. He can see in the dark. He will hear them coming before you."

"Hell. I never fooled with no dog except hunting dogs."

"Her name is Neva. She is more even-tempered than the male. Neva!" The Basque shepherd brought the tall white dog closer and made introductions. Slocum hunkered down for the first sniff, and once the dog wagged its white tail, he fluffed the head between his hands for three or four minutes, talking to it.

"She will attack anything if you point it out and shout to her." Arnaud spoke a Basque word that sounded like "N 'Chay!" The dog's ears pricked, her tail went rigid, and she snarled softly.

"Do not throw her away, señor," the shepherd said.

"I won't. Every minute those sheep aren't moving is a minute lost."

Slocum tied his horse in a grove of pole-sized alders near the place where the trail abandoned the rocky slope and slipped into the meadow. Arnaud had the sheep already moving. Sabrina and Smitty gave Slocum a wave. The dog watched her mate leaving and whined.

Slocum was talking to the animal even as he shed his Colts and cartridge belt. "They don't need you right now, Neva," he said. "I'm the one's gonna be depending on your eyes, because it's getting colder now and that damn sleet will be snow again before we know it." He took his hunter's rifle, the big Sharps single-shot .50 and loaded his pockets with huge bullets. He emptied everything else into his saddlebags, even his tobacco. He'd be on foot up that trail, and his enemies would be on horseback, and he might have to do some fancy stepping.

He went back up the trail, staying above the mud, climbing about as fast as he could. The dog stayed out a hundred yards in front, under his command now, though many of his signals had to be hand signals.

Funny how different it looked on foot, when he'd been on horseback before. And now he was alone. He hurried, and his breathing settled down. He left the trail at the avalanche track, clambering roughly up the slope, which was broken with ankle-turning rocks and debris. He didn't hide his tracks because the snow was covering them for him.

He sat behind a waist-high boulder four hundred yards above the trail. He settled, puffing, and laid his Sharps before him. Him and twelve bullets. Enough to play hell.

He said, "Here's to you, J.D. Murchison."

With the dog beside him, he tipped his hat over his eyes and slept. In common with many other predators, John Slocum could rest whenever and wherever it was needed.

When he woke again, it must have been only fifteen or twenty minutes later, no more. The snow was sticking to the ground, and much of the light seemed to be coming from the snow itself.

It was a long time before his senses confirmed the dog's.

Slocum heard a piece of horse harness jingle, and the first rider came around the bend. Big hombre dressed like a mountain man. He'd been banged around and wasn't riding easy. Must be Teton Jackson. Don't know the others, won't even guess. Ten, twelve, fourteen of them, and now one or two more riding like they're wounded. *Yep. Old J.D. did us some good up there.*

During the war John Slocum had dropped his share of men from ambush. But that was war, and everybody kind of expected it. Now it didn't seem quite fair.

Slocum sighed as he lowered the sights of his Sharps. The big gun roared, and the powder smoke hit the chilled air in a rush, and for the second time today, Teton Jackson's horse was shot away under him.

"Oh Christ!" The horse went over the rim of the trail, punched into oblivion by the Sharps' enormous slug. Jackson clawed his way to the uphill side of the horse and launched himself for safety, which he more or less achieved, though he banged his sore body into the sharp rocks beside the trail. He screamed with pain and rage.

Red Smart had his Colt barking up the slope toward the ambusher's position, which was marked as plain as day by the cloud of smoke.

It was pretty brave, staying on his horse, returning fire, hoping to disrupt the ambusher's aim while the rest of Jackson's bunch got unscrambled. Fourteen men trying to turn their horses on that narrow trail.

The Sharps laid Red Smart's animal across the trail just like a boulder, and a moment later it piled another horse on top.

Three shots at four hundred yards and three good horses were dead—one over the trail. Some of Jackson's band had belly-flopped onto the rock slope and were returning fire. Some were spurring their horses back the way they'd come.

Slocum kept his front sight on his target but held his trigger finger. "Let 'em go. Every damn one of 'em wants to run, I'll let 'em go." The riders were lost in the snow.

Bullets crashed into nearby boulders. The dog lay completely flat.

"Time to skedaddle," Slocum said.

He crawled out behind the boulders, moving quick as he could without showing himself. So long as Jackson's men were shooting boulders, it was fine.

The dog understood the need for concealment, because it stayed in real low and close beside Slocum. The snow was harder now and stung Slocum's cold face when it hit.

Some of Jackson's men were climbing toward Slocum's old position, forming a great arc. Since this morning they'd ridden forty miles, been ambushed twice, and now a hard climb in the snow.

Teton Jackson lay behind a dead horse, furiously pumping lead against the boulders where Slocum had been.

Five hundred yards west, Slocum came to his hands and knees, and now he was running low but erect.

"He ain't up there," Red Smart said, lying beside Jackson, who fired at a crack between two boulders. "The last sonofabitch, he was still up there."

"Yeah, but he was dead meat. Hell, that was old Murchison himself. I never expected to find him up there."

"Well, Teton, whoever was up there is gone, and he killed some of our horses. What we gonna do now? You was in such a god-awful hurry to get here that we ain't got no more spare horses and no packhorses and no grub. And it looks like we're caught in a real blizzard in the high country. Why don't you put your damn rifle down and do some thinking for a change."

Red Smart and Teton Jackson went back a good long way together. Jackson would have killed anyone else for talking to him that way.

He lowered his rifle. Silence of the snow falling. The only warm thing he had was his rifle muzzle, and that'd chill soon enough. His men were staying pretty low. Nobody wanted to be the first target. Jackson heaved himself to his feet. "Come on, you damn fools. Let's get someplace and make camp. Man can't do no good when he's frozen and beat."

Dark falls fast this time of the year, and Jackson's men didn't have the advantage of a dog to guide them. Since they hadn't planned to be wandering around in the night through an unfamiliar forest, nobody had thought to bring a lantern. The snow clotted on their eyebrows and in every crevice of their clothes. They'd been riding hard, and they cooled, and their horses cooled, and they bunched up as they picked their way down the trail in total blackness.

"Who's with us?" Jackson called. He saw horse shapes and man shapes, but that was all. The thickening snow obscured the moon entirely. Jackson tried to put a light to his Havana, but his saddle horn was too damn wet to fire his match.

"You know I'm here," Red Smart said.

"Two Nickle Johnny, yo!"

"Robert Cassidy, and I'm cursing your name, Jackson!"

Pretty soon everybody was accounted for. Eleven men in all. The rest had cut back up the hill into the teeth of the raging blizzard, risking Wyoming and the winter rather than Muleshoe.

"Let's get into the damn trees," Jackson yelled. "Everybody get down and take the tail of the man's horse ahead of you. Let's get ourselves settled in for the night."

And so the band of outlaws proceeded, single file,

deeper into the timber. And it was true—the cedars provided some relief from the blowing weather.

The snow on their face, the temperature, and wind direct on were matters of great concern. Every man knew what it was like getting caught in high country in winter. Hell, it could snow so deep the horses couldn't move. It could leave them stranded up here until spring, just like the Donner Party. And everybody knew the tale of the immigrant party who'd dined on each other until the spring thaw.

Jackson found a clearing where the wind didn't seem to be very bad. He didn't want to wander around in the forest very long because he couldn't see a damn thing, not a thing, and it would be very easy to step his horse off a precipice or into some gully or deadfall. No. He felt his way back over his animal to the next outlaw in the chain. "This is where we camp tonight. First thing we got to do is find firewood."

He told the next man to clear ground for a campfire, and the weary wet outlaw went down on his knees in slush, scrabbling a bare spot. The half-frozen dirt pulled at his fingernails.

Most of the men went for firewood. "Don't get too far from the horses," Jackson said. "If you get lost, fire three shots in the air. Call out; keep calling out."

They found a bull-pine deadfall not fifty feet from the horses, and that was the first piece of luck they'd had this cold and miserable evening. For a wonder, somebody had dry matches. Matches sealed in wax for occasions just like this. Another old hand began whittling some pine tinder.

"Get over here, Red Smart. I need your hat."
Two men knelt over the mound of pine frizzles. The
underside of a stone was the only item dry enough to
spark the match, and with the protection of their
wide-brimmed hats the baby flame took hold.

Jackson's curse. "Goddamn it! How you boys
comin' along with that fire? When she takes off it'll
be like a lighthouse."

"Damn it, hold your water!"

They nursed the pine fire carefully, and men broke
off the bigger limbs to direct the heat.

The fire was in the very lee of the deadfall,
and once it started to roar, an immediate circle of
warmth leapt out at Jackson's miserable riders. The
nearest ones promptly turned their backsides to the
warmth.

Teton Jackson jumped along them with kicks and
punches. "Get clear of that fire. How the hell them
boys out there gonna see it if you're blocking it with
your butts?"

Red Smart whined, "Ah hell, we built it, didn't
we."

"Everybody get back to the fire! Bring what wood
you got!"

Wet snowy shadows stepped into the campfire's
glow.

No more shots. No sound except the mean whis-
tling wind.

Everybody gathered in as close to the heat as they
could get.

Teton Jackson's face was scratched, and his right
arm was stiffening from the hard fall he'd taken

when Slocum killed his horse. He took out his ker-chief to clean his face, and it was wet. Already Jackson's long underwear was wet against his body, and his boots squished when he walked, and one sock had crawled down where it could raise a terrific blister on his heel. He was already limping in anti-cipation.

Red Smart fanned the fire with his hat. The flames licked and charred the wooden backstop and threw great shadows above the deadfall, converting the or-dinary shadows of limbs and shattered trunks into a grotesque forest of shifting shapes.

"Anybody got any dry tobacco?"

Somebody had. The outlaws passed the single pack of Bull Durham from hand to hand protected by a hat.

"Oh Christ, for the life of a highwayman," some-body said, quoting the old Scottish ballad.

"Yeah," Jackson grunted. "I need three men to take care of the horses."

"Now, how we gonna do that?" somebody ob-jected. "There ain't no feed in the saddlebags. Christ, they ain't got a thing—no oats, no bran, no damn thing."

"They got to be rubbed down or we'll have some lungers by dawn." The horses had been run until they were glossy with sweat, and now they were cooling in wet snow. It was the kind of conditions that can create mighty sick horses.

A couple of the outlaws went through the saddle-bags until they found some dry cloths—flour sacks and two Saturday-go-to-town shirts with the gaudy pearl buttons and high-cut collars. They unsaddled the animals and tethered them in a circle. Though the men who owned the fancy shirts bitched like hell, nobody paid them much mind. The horses had to be rubbed down. Riders scuffed the ground snow down to the dead grasses, and the horses lowered their heads to eat. Late-killed winter grass has practically no nutrition in it, but it'd give the horse's stomachs something to do.

Somebody produced a flask and it made the rounds, each man observing protocol and taking just one swallow before passing it to the next man.

"We could build a lean-to," Red Smart said without much enthusiasm for his project.

"Shit," another replied. "I wouldn't go back in those woods for nothing. Until the fire got goin' I was blind as a bat, and even when it was burning I could only see what was between men and the fire. Forget the lean-to."

"Anybody think to pack any grub?" Jackson asked.

Red Smart spat. "If you hadn't been in such a god-awful hurry to hit the trail we could have packed plenty. But you was quick as a hen who's got her tail feathers singed. 'After them, boys!' Shit."

Jackson turned quick. "I don't take that kind of talk from any man, Smart. Now, you take those words back or there's gonna be a fresh corpse by the fire." He laughed. "Haw! Maybe we can eat it."

Somebody tittered, another guffawed, and the tension broke. "No 'fense meant," Smart mumbled. "No 'fense."

"None taken, Red," Jackson said magnanimously.

"The hell with it," somebody said. "I'm gettin' under my damn stinkin' horse blanket and I'm sitting right here by the fire until this weather lets up or until it's morning."

"Where's Cassidy?"

"Cassidy?"

"Yeah. The Mick. Last time I seen him he was goin' out to get wood."

"Cassidy!" The shout went up.

"I'm afraid Mr. Cassidy has gone to his eternal reward," John Slocum said. He jumped up on the big deadfall and both his Colts were in his hands and rock steady. "Cassidy was just lost as hell, and he ran into a certain white dog."

One of the guard dogs jumped up on the deadfall beside him. It was huge-jawed and stiff with the desire to spring. The dog's muzzle was stained a particularly unappealing shade of red.

"Christ almighty," Jackson breathed. He took an involuntary step back and a voice behind halted him.

The voice said, "Listen to John Slocum, señors. There is nothing behind you tonight except death."

Everybody's slicker was drawn tight over their pistols. Most of the outlaws' rifles were with their saddles or put down while their owners warmed themselves.

Teton Jackson was as brave as the next man and probably braver than most. He was also as irritable as a bear. His hands were mighty cold, but he opened the hooks and eyes in his slicker. If a bullet took him, so be it. "Sneakin' around in the dark killin' men," he said. "That ain't no act of a white man.

Stranger, you better hope you got a little Indian blood in you.''

Slocum's lips murmured, ''You better hope you're bullet-proof.''

That froze Teton's hands, but it didn't stop his mouth. ''Who the hell are you, Slocum? Just who the hell are you?''

''We've never met, but a few of your boys and me enjoyed a go-round a few days back.''

''I'm told. So how come you pick a bone with them? Who here has done you harm?''

''I'm a Muleshoe man.''

''Bought and paid for, I'd say.''

''Naw. I'm betting I'll be paid. I haven't had anything out of this little trip yet except for the fun of traipsin' through the hills.''

''What the hell, Slocum? I can see a man workin' for an outfit. Hell I worked for Circle B durin' the Lincoln County wars, and I've worked for a couple other fighting outfits. You had no call to shoot up my place like that. It never had nothing to do with you.''

Another voice from the darkness—an older voice he'd heard before somewhere if he could only think. ''How about the Wolf Kid, Jackson? You backshot him.''

Jackson waved that off. ''It was one of my men did that. An accident.''

Red Smart looked at his boots, admitting nothing.

''You provoked this, pal. You was the first one to throw down on Muleshoe,'' Slocum said.

Two men were having a quiet, reasonable conversation.

A horse nickered.

A second dog slipped up on the deadfall beside Slocum. Like its mate, it was poised to spring, but at least it didn't have any damn blood on its muzzle.

It was hard to look at those dogs without imagining the sharp white fangs closing around some part of your body. The stillness of the two dogs, and John Slocum with his twin Colts. It was enough to make a man think. A couple of Jackson's men eased to the rear, and those who couldn't get behind another man got behind him.

"What about my father?" A woman's voice came from another point on the compass. "J.D. Murchison. You murdered him."

Teton Jackson removed his Stetson and turned toward the voice. "Ma'am, it wasn't no bullet that took Mr. Murchison. He was stone dead when we got to him."

"And I suppose you left him for the wolves?"

Teton Jackson shook his head so vigorously his brains whipped. "No, ma'am. Man like J.D. Murchison deserves a lot of respect. We buried him decent, put a good three feet of rock on top of him so's the wild critters wouldn't unearth him, and I ain't no preacher, ma'am, but I did say a few words over his poor body. He was an honorable man, ma'am, and a hard fighter. Why, if I told you about the poor boys he cut down, it'd make your heart sick, ma'am. He opened up on us without a word, and my good friend Butch went off his horse like a sack of grain. I never had no quarrel with you or your father, ma'am, and I was right sorry to see him dead.'' Teton Jackson inclined his huge body toward the darkness. He expressed mute appeal. His own memory had forgotten the splash old Murchison's body had made on the rocks where he'd been hurled. He had invented ancient friendship and mutual respect, and, by God, he believed his own illusion.

''Ma'am, we came up here to clear up our misunderstanding. I suppose the families of the boys Mr. Murchison shot down would like burial expenses, but I'm sure we could forgo that.''

Slocum grinned from ear to ear. God, he loved a man who could perform in tight spots. ''And I suppose you never objected to Muleshoe sheep on this trail. I suppose you never said nothing about leavin' 'em to starve.''

Jackson didn't see anyone from that time. He took his chance. ''Whoever told you that is a dirty liar.''

They all listened to the snowfall. It patted men's clothes. It hissed when it hit the fire. It was so quiet you could almost hear the drops sliding off Jackson's slicker.

Teton Jackson held his breath.

Smitty, the belly robber, came out of the trees holding his long-barreled J.W. Dance revolver at his side.

The old belly robber walked with the fastidiousness of a man who didn't care to get slush on his boots. With the pistol in his hands he looked capable, and at first Teton Jackson didn't recognize the frightened man he'd faced down before Red Smart shot the Kid.

''It wasn't like you said,'' Smitty said. ''You told us you'd kill anybody come to move those sheep.''

Jackson tried his best smile. "Hell, *compadre*, anybody can make a little mistake."

"Big mistake, if I'm any judge," Smitty said.

"So, all right. We thought we was treein' squirrels, and it turned out they were bobcats. I been followin' your tracks all damn day. You got three men riders and at least one woman. Those dogs are the hounds of hell, but I never seen no dog could stand up to a flat-nosed .44 slug. Put a couple pills in those bastards and they won't be killin' no more of my men. There's ten of us standin' here, and that's odds of three to one, no matter how lucky you get."

"I hope the world you're heading to will suit you as well as the one you presently enjoy," John Slocum said, with his mild smile. One of his Colts was aimed at Jackson's brain.

Jackson licked his lips. "So be it," he said. "I don't get backed down, John Slocum. I come out to this country in the first place because I wanted room to move, and I keep that room any way I can."

"Seven feet long, three feet wide, seventy-seven inches deep. That's how much room you'll occupy, Jackson."

Jackson's nerve broke. The eye of that Colt was one too much for him. He raised his hand in the air. "Now, damn it, let's work a horse trade, Slocum. I never heard you was an unreasonable man. I always heard you'd give a man a fair shake. You got a few pals and a hell of a lot of sheep, and if it keeps on snowin' you're gonna have as much trouble getting down out of this country as we are. Here's what I propose. I propose we let bygones be bygones. We can ride down together."

Slocum didn't think that was such a bad idea if Jackson's men were willing to turn in their weapons; that'd end the bloodshed. Slocum didn't figure Jackson would bother Muleshoe again.

Things would have turned out differently if Slocum had accepted Teton Jackson's offer right away, but he took a few minutes to think, and Smitty got restless and recognized Red Smart and said, "I don't believe you should live, you damn backshooter. The hell with you," and put two bullets into Red Smart's liver.

9

Red Smart folded over like a notecard with his mouth wide open for all the sounds he wasn't making. Blood gushed out of his mouth, and his eyes were terribly pained like he was embarrassed about the blood and wished he didn't have to do it.

Even then it might have stopped, but Teton Jackson had had enough. The bullet Smitty triggered, triggered him. Jackson dove to the side, just away from the fire, and as he dove, his hand went under his slicker. He didn't take the time to unbutton it.

He landed so hard it knocked the air out of him and crushed his hand under his weight, and he rolled over on his back like a fish with his boot tips pointing straight to the sky. His hat spun off him and rolled into the snow, and his greasy hair flopped around as he tried desperately to free his weapon—as agonized as a man reaching for his cock when he knows he's just going to piss himself if he doesn't get the damned thing out.

Slocum fired once and killed a man. He fired again and missed a man who was lifting a rifle to his hip with truly surprising speed. This gunfighter moved as fast as any of the men Slocum had ridden with during the war. The rifle just seemed to jump into the man's hands, and it so startled John Slocum that the bullet he meant for the man's heart snipped a chunk of cloth from the man's shirt at the armpit.

The gunman's return fire was the first sign that Jackson's men were fighting back. It burned the air over Slocum's chest as he did a back flip off the big piece of dead wood. Damn! A man could get killed in this line of work.

The dogs hit the gunman low and high, but not before he'd levered another slug into the long gun and cranked off number two.

He was a fair-haired man with a large, bulbous forehead, and his face simply fell away to nothing at his chin. His teeth were quite terrible—it looked like some child had thrown them into his mouth—and the best teeth he had were the ones he'd had pulled, because every time he opened his mouth he seemed to be biting his cheeks. His lank blond hair hung down the right-hand side of his face. His right arm was four inches longer than his left arm, and he had enormous hands with broad spatulate fingers.

His bullet killed the dog who was coming in low. The bullet hit the charging animal's chest and went quite through him and took all life out with it.

A dog body crashed into the gunman's knees as the high dog hugged his face and took a bite.

The gunman screamed. Another of Jackson's men was burning powder now, his bullets searching the air where Slocum had been.

Unmoved by all this, Smitty stared at the man he'd so easily killed. He wore the slightly satisfied smile of a trophy hunter with a prize rack. The J.W. Dance pistol hung from his hand, forgotten.

Slocum had fallen into the deadfall. His head cracked into a hard resiny nub and his left hand opened, like the two points were connected in his body, and he lost the gun. He clutched his other pistol and half rolled and groaned. His head was full of billowing red clouds, and he squinched down against the pain.

Mary Anne Murchison had been standing well back inside the trees. She'd heard some of what was said and missed more of it. She never did hear what Smitty said to Red Smart, so she didn't know why the fight started. She was glad it was started though. She wasn't going to sleep well at night until every one of Jackson's varmints was killed or mashed like the filthy insects they were. Resolutely, she began firing the Smith & Wesson she carried. But she fired at random.

Teton Jackson fired, rolled, fired again, and scrambled out of the damn firelight.

John Slocum threw up. Crowded down between the branches of the tree, with his ears ringing from the blow he'd taken, he got god-awful sick. He'd shaken his brains loose.

With his left hand he dragged on the damn deadfall and tried to pull himself to a sitting position. To him, sitting seemed like the most important thing in the world.

Most of Jackson's men were fighting. Hell, what choice had they?

Since Smitty wasn't offering any particular threat, after he'd taken his revenge for the Wolf Kid, maybe Jackson's boys might have left him alone, but they were at war with a vengeance and a small-caliber bullet cracked into Smitty's hip. It was as if a hammer had hit him—the sudden crushing force of it.

Since the bullet was small, it didn't push Smitty over, it just jolted him. Another two or three from the same small handgun missed clear.

Smitty eyed his wound, his mouth agape with surprise. Oh hell. It wasn't supposed to work like that. It wasn't fair. The world owed him one dead man anyway, after taking his family during the war, and now his pal. And what about old Murchison? Smitty had liked him, too.

A bullet blew into the side of his foot where it broadened into the ankle. Smitty's boot took a little of the shock, but the bullet just splashed through, and his foot spouted bone and then blood. He saw his foot explode. That angered him. He meant to do something about it. The Dance lifted in his hand. His angry thumb dropped the hammer on a cap so old it wouldn't fire.

One of Mary Anne's stray slugs took the old cook in the chest, and he lost all his wind all at once, and when he tried to drag in air he couldn't. And then breathing or not breathing became somewhat abstract questions. He knew his pistol was falling from his nerveless hand, and he knew his legs were crumpling, and he simply didn't care.

Though it was Mary Anne's misfired bullet that took him, it might just as well have been bullets from other Jackson killers, who were smoking pretty hard now, weaving a tapestry of bullets, like magicians, each inscribing his zone of influence.

The blond gunman had his throat chomped out by the big white guard dog. Inside he was screaming, but nobody could hear a word. His head was thrown back in an awful manner, and men looked away from a wound they didn't wish to see.

John Slocum poked one Colt over that deadfall and slipped the hammer. Killed a man. Through his misty red vision he could see his man fall.

The horses were going crazy. Stray bullets zipped among them, and one animal was already wounded.

Jackson's men were on the inside of a circle, except for Jackson himself, who fired from the woods.

Arnaud fired both barrels of his scattergun. Arnaud's eyes were big and wide, and he dropped his scattergun in the snow and stepped into the firelight with only knife in hand. He and the guard dog went for the same man. The man was firing his banker's Colt at the dog, but the dog was weaving, and he wasn't having any luck, and the dog was bounding awful close.

Arnaud slammed into his man from the side, with his knife going up and in and the other man's sweaty terrified face inches from his own as the Basque rode him down.

Sabrina shot a man who grabbed at his stomach and walked around groaning until he ran into the man with no throat and flattened him for the last time. The throatless gunfighter's heels started drumming the earth, like a child in a tantrum, but there was nothing that man wanted ever again.

Teton Jackson drew a careful bead and blew the dog off his pal. As Arnaud turned, Jackson fired again. It gave him enormous satisfaction to see a Muleshoe man go down under his gun. He tried Slocum. Just Slocum's face and Colt showed above his wooden barricade, and Slocum fired at the muzzle flash that had tried him on for size.

Sabrina bolted into the firelight after her brother. She sobbed her hysteria in Basque then, the language of her soul, a speech that cried out about the injustice of God to man.

Two of Jackson's men still stood. One wore an enormous wolf-fur parka, and the other was as slight as a boy. Slocum's bullet crashed into his wrist. Teton Jackson fired again at Sabrina, but his bullet lodged in her already dead brother. The dog had been gut-shot and dragged himself around with his forepaws digging through the snow.

Some of Jackson's horses pulled their tethers and ran into the night.

Jackson dropped his hammer on an empty chamber and cursed. If he'd had powder under his hammer, he would have dropped the girl for sure.

It didn't really seem worth it. Men crashing into trees, heading in his direction. Two of his men weren't firing any more than Jackson was and ducked when John Slocum cranked off a couple in their direction.

Except for Sabrina's sobbing and the sound as the hurt dog dragged himself along, the campsite was quiet.

Mary Anne's face was exultant. She smacked her hand into her fist. "We won," she whispered. Encouraged by the silence that followed her first remark, she shouted, "We won, God help us, we beat them! My father is avenged!"

Slocum climbed on the log. One hand held his Colt, the other was pressed against the side of his head. "Oh yeah, we showed 'em all right."

The belly-shot man walked toward Mary Anne, beads of agony-sweat on his forehead. Mary Anne retreated. The man had voided himself, and the stink was quite unpleasant. That stink and the stink of freshly spilled blood, the smell of opened guts, and the reek of black powder.

The snow fell steadily, as able to cover the dead as the living. The campfire popped and sputtered, as happy as any other fire, unconcerned with the fate of its makers.

John Slocum holstered his Colt.

Mary Anne marched around the clearing like a general inspecting a victorious battlefield. Teton Jackson stood out in the cold, watching her and hating this little woman and too afraid to reload his Colt and begin again.

Steadily the dog crawled toward the forest, where it meant to die.

Slocum took the belly-shot man's arm and sat him down in the snow. He grabbed one of Jackson's saddles and a couple of the heavy horse blankets and laid them over the hurt man.

"Say, pard, you ain't got a drop of whiskey?"

Slocum shook his head. He had a couple of bottles back at their camp, but when they'd come out tonight to hit Jackson's camp they hadn't brought any.

"I sure would like a nip," the man said vaguely.

"You ain't supposed to give nothing to men who been gut-shot," Slocum said, remembering from the war.

"Oh hell," the man said. "I ain't gonna live long anyway. I'm just as dead as Old Red Smart. I surely want to have me some whiskey."

Slocum went through the saddlebags, and it wasn't long before he found a pint bottle in among some rider's long underwear.

He took a nip and handed it to the hurt man. After his Adam's apple bobbed, he said, "Oh God that hurts."

Slocum reached for the bottle, but the man hung onto it.

"It hurts, but it hurts good," he explained.

Mary Anne was doing a dance. It reminded Slocum of the scalp dance Crow squaws did whenever they were turned loose on a battlefield. Mary Anne danced up to each of the enemy dead and touched them with her boot toe. When she thought nobody was watching, she stomped on one dead man's fingertips, grinding them into the snowy ground.

"Mary Anne!" Slocum called.

She raised her eyebrows in a question. She wasn't doing anything wrong.

No sense in explaining it to her. "Get on over here, Mary Anne. We might get back to our own camp and get what sleep we can. We still got a big flock of sheep to take care of."

Sabrina lifted her tear-streaked face. "My brother?"

"We'll come back here in the morning." He paused. "Arnaud . . . he'd do."

"He was so brave, so good. And they cut him down!" She screamed again, and this time her cry was like the shriek of a predator. She shook her fist at the darkness outside the fire where Jackson and his survivors lay low. "You will not live," she shouted. "Sabrina Oleacharga can promise you that."

And so violent was her cry that Jackson and his

men shivered. The skinny youth with the shot wrist softly moaned. Jackson tied him a tourniquet with his neckerchief.

Jackson's blood was running colder now, and he knew they needed that fire. A few hours out here in this snowfall and, by God, they'd freeze to death. He watched John Slocum toss more wood on the fire. He saw Sabrina pleading with Slocum, who clearly didn't want to do whatever it was she was asking and shook his head no three times before he shook it yes.

"Jackson!" Slocum called.

Jackson stayed quiet. The man in the wolf-fur coat drew it closer about his body, and the skinny man whimpered.

"I could douse this fire and leave you all out there with no way to live through the night. I could douse this fire and kill you all, sure as a bullet to your head."

Sabrina was at him again with her whispered request. It had something to do with the hurt dog she'd brought back beside the fire.

"I'll leave the fire, and I'll leave your pal, Jackson. I'm gonna scatter your horses, because it'll slow you down. I don't want no more trouble with you, Jackson. I done killed as many as I wished to."

Slocum went to the remaining tethered horses then and drove them out into the woods, stinging them with Teton Jackson's own personal quirt when they were unwilling.

Because Sabrina wanted it, he hoisted the hurt dog across his shoulders before he and his two women companions left the campsite.

The snow fell into the fire and softened the outline

of the dead men's clothes. It melted where it touched their hot blood and their warm flesh, but it'd win before the night was out, and it had plenty of patience.

Sabrina called to the two herding dogs, who barked hysterically when they heard her voice, and beckoned them into their own snug camp.

Built in the lee of a great boulder, the fire was invisible until you were almost on top of it. The buckboard was drawn in close and soogans were spread out as invitingly as a bed.

John Slocum laid the wounded dog down with the two herding dogs. The hurt animal frightened them, and they backed far away before they came in closer to identify their comrade. Their busy tongues were soon cleaning his face and fur.

Before they had set out for their attack, Smitty had created a mulligan stew—scraps of meat, carrots, and potatoes—and now it burbled in a pot beside the fire.

John Slocum knelt to fill three plates with stew. "I can't eat," Sabrina said. "My brother is dead." She spoke with the simple peasant dignity that precedes a period of mourning.

But this wasn't her home country, and Slocum's voice cracked roughly as he ordered, "Eat what you can. If you can't eat, drink the damn broth. We're gonna need you tomorrow, Sabrina."

Her honest face. "He was such a good man."

John Slocum had seen more than his share of good men dead. "Eat your stew," he said. "You must."

Mary Anne's cheeks were still flushed with the excitement of it all. She could probably develop a taste for this sort of thing. Right now she was

wishing she was a man, because men get to
this all the time.

She didn't have much of an appetite either, but she
ate her stew like a good little soldier.

"Take a tarp and your soogans out from the wagon,
Mary Anne," Slocum said.

"Why? There's room enough. There's more room
under there now."

The wounded dog lay still, its tongue lolling out.
Only the movements of its flanks showed the life still
coursing in its veins.

Mary Anne moved her gear out of the wagon.

She stared into the fire from a new angle as John
Slocum and Sabrina stripped and got under their
blankets. Their blankets were side by side. Mary
Anne Murchison thought, *Today I have lost my father, and yet he does not comfort me. Today I am
alone in the world, and John Slocum lies down with
a dark girl, a foreign girl, rather than me. It is not
right. It is not fair.* Her eyes burned bright with
anger.

Sabrina lay in John Slocum's arms, her body burning with fever. Her eyes were distant and vague, and
the whites were yellow, and her cheeks were fevered
and dry.

Her body pressed against Slocum's, and her pubic
hair rubbed against his belly like bristles, and her
breasts were flattened against his chest, and her arms
were around his back, pulling him tight to her fever,
her hurt.

"He was a good man," she murmured in his ear.
Then, in her own language, she told her tale about
her brother. How it had been in the country where

ow they'd grown up, wilder than
happiest with their animals under
h the ocean below, pale, pale blue,
f the hillside as white as snow. They
country because . . . because. . . .
because it was their time, and because
they w ready for new ways in a new land. Their
pride was their grubstake—that and their knowledge
of sheep. They traveled through the country, ever
west, looking for the skies of their homeland. And
they had found those skies, and their work and their
happiness, and now Arnaud was dead. Dead. Oh, he
was dead!

John Slocum didn't understand a word. Her heart
was thudding against his, and her flesh was as hot as
a furnace now, burning her grief into her bone.

"It shouldn't have happened," he said. "I meant
for us to send them packing. It would have worked,
too."

Sabrina told him about her brother's endearing
character and dissolved in tears. Tears and more tears
wet her cheeks and her neck and ran down where
their bodies were close together and cooled her, and
she turned into moisture, cleansing her grief, cooling
herself, finding the life that is moisture.

It was neither love nor lust that planted John Slocum inside the strange Basque girl. It was not need
that drew him into her.

She was a virgin and parted slowly before him,
cooling his entryway. He didn't move his hips, he
simply grew within her, and she opened for him to
let him in.

She felt a tiny twinge, like regret.

He grew until he filled her up, until she could let her sorrow marry his, and they became, for a long moment, the ones who were each other.

They fell asleep that way.

At first light John Slocum woke with Sabrina at his back and Mary Anne Murchison's furious face not inches from his. Her eyes were as round as two-bit pieces and just as shiny. Her fists were clenched at her side.

John Slocum moistened his lips. "Mornin'," he croaked.

She was speechless with rage. No telling how long she'd been squatting there, watching the two of them sleep. Slocum wrinkled up his face. "Is that bacon I smell frying?" he asked.

Mary Anne's face found a smile. "I think you can feed yourself, cowboy. I'm not your fucking slave."

Slocum scratched his head.

The fire was still good. He supposed Mary Anne had fed it during the night. Gave him the creeps, her prowling around that way while he slept. No telling what that one might decide to do.

Six inches worth of snow. The sky was bright but overcast. There wasn't enough sun to melt this stuff.

Slocum came out of the blankets and got into his longjohns. Mary Anne deliberately turned away from his nakedness, stiff as a poker.

Carefully, she emptied the frying pan of its precisely sliced three slices of bacon and ate them, every one. They tasted like ashes in her mouth, but she was bound and determined to finish every bite.

When Slocum had his boots on, he made a quick circle around the camp with his rifle in his hand looking for signs of Jackson and company. Nope. They'd stayed back at their own campfire.

The wounded dog lay where it had been. Its eyes were glazing. Its sides heaved.

"Well," Slocum said, "we did him no good bringing him here."

From her blankets Sabrina said, "But I wanted so much to help someone—something."

"Sure," Slocum said. The dog breathed its last, and the two herding dogs gave it a good sniff before backing away from the corpse.

Sabrina cooked breakfast for herself and Slocum. She rarely spoke to Slocum and hardly noticed Mary Anne Murchison at all.

Once she'd finished eating, Mary Anne rode out to the flock. Four thousand animals had cleared a fair patch of ground, and the sheep were yarded up. As soon as they saw the rider, they bleated eagerly, because all the older ewes knew that when the weather turned snowy, humans were bound to appear with their hay.

When she got to the camp, she said, "Slocum, the animals are ready to move, right now. If we get a good start, we can be down on the Camas at noon."

Slocum washed the frying pan in snow. The buckboard was packed up and ready to roll. "I figured we'd gather up our dead before we drove down. Ground's too hard to bury 'em here, and Sabrina doesn't want no Indian burial platform."

"And my father?"

"Well, Teton Jackson said he buried him good, but if you want, we can go back up there and dig him up and bring him down too. We can wait to drive until tomorrow morning, and if those snowy-lookin' clouds don't hold no snow in their bellies, then we ought to get down all right.''

"Forget him," she sneered. "After all, he was just the man who hired you.''

"Mary Anne, if you want we can go back up there and—''

"I said forget him!''

Sabrina drove the buckboard and Slocum rode flanker. Jackson was still armed and dangerous, and he had left signs at his campsite. From the marks, he and three men had camped right next to the fire all night, and in the morning their bootprints went east— the direction Slocum had driven their horses.

They'd stripped the corpses of watches and money belts. Every dead man's pocket was open and inside out, and they'd cut away Arnaud's gold crucifix.

They'd left their pal, the belly-shot man, wrapped in the same blankets Slocum had wrapped him in last night.

"You look like hell," Slocum said, bending close.

"Thanks," he breathed. "You got any more of that whiskey? Those bastards never left me a drop.''

Slocum opened a fresh pint and held the bottle to the wounded man's mouth. When he spoke again, the hurt man was stronger. "You can do me one more favor, pal.''

"Yeah?''

"Sure. Give me another drink of that whiskey, and if I don't drown, then you kill me, *comprendo*?''

"We was thinkin' of takin' you down in the buckboard. We'll be back at Muleshoe by nightfall.''

"Ah, what's the use. It'll hurt like hell goin' down

that trail, and I ain't gonna make it anyway. I got to tell you, you ain't likely to celebrate too many more birthdays either. Teton Jackson sat beside the fire last night and didn't sleep a wink, and he cursed you with some of the most horrible curses a man'd ever want to hear. Oh, he means to take a piece of you, believe me that. Now, I got this appointment over the River Jordan. So you just do me that favor, pard, and send me on my way.''

''Pleasure knowing you,'' Slocum said, and tilted the bottle again. The man closed his eyes while drinking, and something like a beatific expression crossed his face, transforming it into the kind of pilgrim one does expect to see crossing the Jordan.

Before he'd finished the bottle, Slocum killed him. The shot clapped.

Slocum wondered if Jackson and his men had heard it. Probably not. Sound gets kind of muffled after a fresh snowfall. Slocum didn't look again at the man he'd killed, not once. He loaded the two bodies on the wagon. Teton Jackson or the wolves could inter their dead. John Slocum took care of his own.

The little herding dogs had their work cut out starting the flock. Time and again the sheep balked while the little herders hurled themselves at their heels, yipping and snapping. When the flock finally slid into motion it was like a great wave breaking. While the meadow was broad, Slocum rode wide. He came upon Jackson's hoofprints almost immediately. They'd caught three horses and were heading out as directly as they could. From the length of the stride, he guessed they were in a hurry. He didn't think they'd try anything today. They'd lick their wounds for a couple of days before they got dangerous again.

When the valley narrowed, Slocum dropped back to the rear. Sabrina followed the buckboard, which Mary Anne Murchison was driving. A blue wool blanket covered Smitty, and a Navaho blanket disguised Arnaud's form without concealing it. The dogs kept the sheep plowing ahead.

The three riders were silent, in separate worlds. For the time being they'd said what they could.

The sky hung over the river of sheep like a dark wet promise. At any moment the clouds could open and drop more snow.

The sheep marched onto the narrower trail—not so much different from the one they'd walked yesterday. From time to time an older sheep fell beside the trail. The dogs got some of these to their feet.

The sun crawled along behind the clouds. Blotches of light showed its progress. A couple of crows jumped out of the trees beside the trail. Black dots in the sky.

Though he wasn't real hungry, John Slocum pulled over at noon. Neither of the women was hungry either. Slocum forced himself to eat a couple of the dead cook's biscuits. They flaked in his mouth.

They continued, the sun continued, the season deepened, and it started to snow. A brisk competent snow, it meant to cover the earth—that was its business.

The lead sheep stepped out onto the Camas Prairie and were so delighted at the familiar ground and the familiar foodstuff that they spread out on the vast plain to paw the snow and graze. Most of the camas is underground, stored in the roots; the leaves and winter-killed tops are prime fodder.

Slocum dozed in the saddle. His horse knew what to do, and God, Slocum was tired.

The snow fringed the riders, turned the bodies into mounds, covered sleeves, hats, the traces, even the brasses on the horse bridles. It closed down the world again as sure as a sandstorm, and the dogs kept the expanding flock on the path by constant circling. Sabrina rode with the dogs, doing a more active job of herding now.

Slocum drowsed. His eyes closed down, heavy as sash weights. Behind his shuttered eyes he dreamed. The snow caught on his collar, but John Slocum was back in the Grizzly Bear Saloon on a Saturday night with a good crowd at the bar and a laughing girl at his elbow.

Slocum had learned the knack of dozing through interminable miles, and now he relived the gaiety and the music he'd known at the Grizzly Bear Saloon and all the other places he'd passed good times in. He dreamed of the women he'd known—the joking ones, the quiet ones, the sweet ones; the women he'd conquered, the women who had conquered him. Faces floated in his memory.

The wind swung around and came at them from the northwest, riding all the way down from the Canadian line. It filled the sheep's wool, and the dogs had to leave more sheep behind.

Mary Anne Murchison looked over the sheep and her heart was full of hatred. John Slocum had comforted the wrong woman. And she, Mary Anne, was wronged—badly wronged.

Her thoughts pursued circles like the snake that eats its own tail—a rage that feeds on itself and burns the human spirit that gives that hatred room.

Mary Anne thought about Renfrew, the foreman whose mistake had got them into this thing in the first place. The passage of time had been kind to this gent in Mary Anne's memory; he had taken on certain characteristics that hadn't seemed to count for much before: Renfrew was steady. Renfrew wasn't sticky with blood. Renfrew was devoted to her. Devoted.

Slocum rode beside Sabrina, awake, bone weary.

Together they raced to the left or right, helping the dogs keep the sheep on course. The trail became a road, straight as a die. The animals stayed pretty much within its shoulders, guided.

During a moment when everything was working right for a change, Sabrina asked, "What will you do when this work is finished?"

He shrugged. "There's still Jackson, you know. I got some bad feelings about this whole affair, but I got especially bad feelings about him. He's gonna want vengeance. Afterwards . . ." He shrugged.

"You do not wish to say, because you think you will be dead."

"Thinking that way's what keeps you alive," Slocum said, which was true enough, but not the sort of thing he said to most people.

"I could not live that way," Sabrina said briskly. "The flock we follow will eat through the winter, and in the spring those who have survived will have their lambs, and these lambs, they will gather together, twenty, fifty, a hundred of them in a group and rush about the pasture, skipping and dancing, and that is nothing more than the pure joy of being alive. I know there are more births than deaths.''

''Yeah,'' Slocum said. He fumbled deep underneath his slicker for some tobacco. There wasn't much left, and he had to lean almost flat in the saddle to get his quirly rolled and lit. He took a deep puff. He said, ''These quirlys take your wind and your appetite, but it's a real pleasure the way they can give a man time to think. I suppose you're right. There's been too much dying on my backtrail. I suppose another man would have made decisions different and jumped to the left when I jumped to the right. There's dozens of times I could have trod the straight and narrow. There's been honest jobs offered. I could have been a stage driver or a horse breaker. Man in Kansas wanted me to honcho his ranch, and it was a damn big ranch too—five thousand head of longhorns, some of those new English Hereford cattle, and two hundred Duroc pigs. I told the man 'No thanks.' He said, 'Why was it?' and I said it was because of the pigs. 'Damn it, man,' he said, 'I'll sell the pigs. They're just a hobby of mine.' I said, 'Thanks, but you're gonna be better off with the pigs. If there ain't no trouble tracking me down, I go into town on Saturday night and find it.' ''

Sabrina mocked. ''What a good life, Mr. Slocum. You take pleasure in your family and are devoted to your work. You have the respect and friendship of your neighbors. Sometimes men come to you for help, and often you give it to them. That is what we call a 'don.' 'Don Slocum.' Ah. The name does not suit you.''

Slocum grinned at her. "You betcha," he said. "If those sheep take the north fork ahead, we'll be in trouble again."

But Sabrina wasn't quite through with John Slocum, and she was just as quick as he was, so the two of them galloped past the astonished, plodding sheep, horse hooves tossing snow plumes, the weary horses slowing of their own accord.

For a moment, on that ride, Slocum felt the clean new life he could have with this woman. For a moment he felt its pull.

An hour later, with the sun pulling its cloak, Slocum dismounted to open Muleshoe's gate. An ordinary cast-off mule shoe hung on the crossbar above the gate. It had meant something to Murchison. Slocum thought it was odd how you keep on getting acquainted with a man when he's dead.

They sent the dogs on to turn the sheep at the pasture gates. The older ewes hurried into the familiar pasture with glad bleats.

Mary Anne went to the house, leaving Slocum and Sabrina to push the sheep through the last gate. The dogs lay beside the gate, completely exhausted. One of them had torn his foot and had left bloody pawprints for the last five miles. He licked his wound. The sheep flowed through, gray, as the light waned. When the last of them passed through, they were black shadows, bustle and noise. Slocum hooked the wire fastener over the gate and said, "So."

"Yes. So."

Slocum remounted, and Sabrina called the dogs onto their feet.

The windows of the ranch headquarters glowed

their invitation. The whole house was ablaze with life. Slocum groaned. First the horse, then the man: a harsh motto the wise man obeyed absolutely.

"You go on in," Slocum said. "I'll rub down the horses."

The horse barn was blessedly dry and full of horses. None of them had recently been ridden hard. Slocum stripped off the harnesses and removed the bridles from their mouths. The horses rolled their jaws, ridding themselves of the weight. He found some feed sacks, and he took his time rubbing them down. He fitted them with nose buckets and just one scoop of oats. No sense hitting them too hard with grain all at once. He forked some fine timothy hay into the stalls and pumped their water.

The bright rectangles of the house were very inviting, so John Slocum tiptoed around on the porch and peeked in the windows before he straightened himself, cursed himself for bein' a spooky kid, and went inside.

10

Past the room where a man could hang his coat, the Muleshoe opened into the broad room where old J.D. had practically lived the last months of his life. There were plenty of signs of the sick man, but John Slocum didn't have time to inventory them because the foreman, Renfrew, was marching toward him with the look on his face that only two creatures wear—a bull sizing you up and a man on the rampage. Ten feet away, he was already cocking his fist. Slocum had never met Renfrew before. Renfrew was one of the Muleshoe's hands, so why did he have his haymaker ready?

Behind him he saw Mary Anne Murchison peeking through the kitchen doorway and wearing the expression of a child enjoying something forbidden.

"You bastard. You scoundrel!" Renfrew used those words and threw his punch. It huffed and puffed as it came through the air, picking up speed. Slocum had seen drunks throw slower punches, but they had been mighty drunk.

He stepped to the side and it whistled past his ear and he grabbed Renfrew's arm and helped it along its way. What steam Renfrew hadn't put into it, Slocum did, and Renfrew punched a deer antler and quite shattered a quaint coatrack and did his knuckles no good. He yelped.

Slocum pulled his Colt and said, "I am too weary for games. Come at me again and I'll arrange your funeral."

Well, Renfrew cursed and held his hurt hand and his eyes were mad clean through. "You can't do that, you bastard! Nobody can do that to a decent woman!"

Mary Anne had vanished. She'd just stayed long enough to see her mischief fail.

"Son, I don't know what the hell you're talkin' about, and I ain't in any big hurry to find out. That's the second time you alleged that my mamma and daddy wasn't wed. They was. I seen their wedding picture many, many times. I been shot at, run at, and beat up. I've been in the snow too long, and I've smelled more damn blood than I care to remember. If you want to die, keep on comin'."

And with that, John Slocum holstered his Colt and leaned past Renfrew to hang his slicker on the horn the foreman had broken. He joined Sabrina beside the roaring fire. He stuck his hands out. "Who the hell is that well-fed hombre?"

"He is the Muleshoe foreman. His name is Jack Renfrew, and I think Miss Murchison can wrap him around her little finger."

The flames whooped up the chimney. It was a real blaze, river-bottom ash hardwood, and the warmth baked him.

"The more I see of humankind, the more I understand why the bear sleeps all winter. Nine months of this world is about all a man can take before he naturally falls into a snooze.''

''Are you so very different from the rest of us?''

''Hell no! That's what worries me. You know, I could have elected to handle it some other way. I didn't have to go helling into Jackson's roadhouse. If we'd just gone about our business we could have got those sheep off the mountain before Jackson come back from Wyoming. A few more men'd be alive right now if that had been how I'd elected to do it.''

She put her hand on his arm. ''We all had choices, every step of the way.''

''But Arnaud . . .''

Her grip tightened up until she gripped bone. ''I will not have you thinking about Arnaud,'' she hissed. ''He is dead because a bullet killed him. It was no bullet of yours but an enemy bullet. If you say you killed my brother, then I must kill you myself.'' Oh, she was mad as hell. She'd smelled Slocum's self-pity.

Slocum's slow, tired grin. ''Thanks,'' he said.

For reply she squeezed his arm again, more kindly this time.

When Slocum turned to warm his other side, Renfrew was slumped in old J.D.'s big leather chair. The chair dwarfed the foreman. He glowered.

''Jesus Christ, fella, what have I ever done to offend you?''

''Miss Murchison, that's who.''

''So? What about her?''

''You defiled her!''

''In the first place, she defiled real easy, and

second, I don't know how it's any concern of yours. You're the foreman of this spread?''

"I'm in charge. Mary Anne—Miss Murchison—told me about the old man. Oh, he was a real heller, he was.''

"He fought well at the end. I guess he was happy to go out fighting for his ranch.''

"Well, since the boss is gone, I guess I'm in charge. Unless Mary Anne tells me different.''

"You been here by yourself now, what? Three weeks, about that?''

"Just about.''

"Well, you sure as hell found the pantry.'' Renfrew had a wide belt of blubber around his waist. He blushed. While Mary Anne had been gone he'd lain around the ranchhouse. Once a day he'd fed the horses and let 'em out in the pasture for exercise. Once a day he'd rounded them up and put them back in the barn. Every day he'd gone into Smitty's pantry, seeking the jams the old man had laid up, the pork tenderloins he'd canned, even the wee bit of fresh sorghum syrup the belly robber had been saving for a special occasion.

With ill grace, Renfrew went to the liquor cabinet. "Old J.D'd offer you a drink. It must have been pretty tough back there.''

Slocum eyed the bottle with some distaste. He said, "I'd take a drink from old J.D. I don't know you from a hole in the wall.''

Renfrew put the whiskey back, as sullen as before.

"Since you're the honcho here, you better know some things. I don't know what Mary Anne's been spillin' and I don't care. You got four thousand woolies out there . . ."

"Four thousand? When I started driving them, there was eight."

"If you'd kept on driving, maybe the wolves wouldn't have eaten half of them. What the hell possessed you to back down before Teton Jackson? He ain't much. What the hell are you made of?"

Renfrew had the grace to look away. "He had the drop on us."

"Yeah. I'll bet he did. Next time it comes to fightin' for the Muleshoe, you better get behind Miss Murchison where you'll be safe. Now"—and John Slocum rolled right past the offense he was causing— "four thousand sheep. I hope to God you got some feed for 'em. I hope you got some pens. I hope you're ready."

Renfrew allowed as how he was.

"Good. Me and the lady will be stayin' for a week."

"You can leave in the morning."

"Nothin' I'd rather do. Teton Jackson and two pals are in that damn storm somewhere, and I reckon their bellies are growling and they're mad enough to chew nails. Muleshoe's the only ranch for sixty miles north or south. Where do you expect he'll come?"

"You've brought Teton Jackson here?" Renfrew was incredulous. Renfrew had gotten used to being alone—alone in his work, alone in the big house, sitting in the old man's chair, drinking his whiskey and smoking his cigars. "You're the devil!" he blurted.

"I never hung out the welcome mat for Jackson," Slocum observed.

Renfrew was at the big glass rifle case. He plucked J.D.'s own Spencer carbine from the collection of weapons.

"I'll take first watch," he said.

"You do that," Slocum replied. "You can have the second and the third watch too. Any man wakes me up tonight will die, whether it's you or Jackson. Good night."

Slocum walked into the back part of the house, opening doors until he found a bedroom. It was old J.D.'s bedroom. Slocum didn't know that. He was too goddamned beat to care. The long walls were very slightly blurry at the edges and the floor was tossing a bit. He slumped on the foot of the bed.

Sabrina was in the doorway. She said, "I will not sleep with you tonight, John."

He looked at her face for a moment, drinking her in. He said, "You come and go as you please."

She pleased to go.

He got his boots off, and by the greatest labor he got his pants off too. His clothes were filthy and lay sodden on the polished floor. John Slocum propped a chair against the doorknob, put a Colt under the pillow, and covered himself. He felt the familiar comfort of cold steel warming under his hand. By morning the Colt would be warm and pleasant, but it took time for steel to get warm.

He slept until ten. Renfrew was shouting and carrying on outside somewhere. He thought he heard Mary Anne Murchison hollering too. He stretched his frame in the big soft bed. Alive. He was alive and in the strength of his manhood. What could be better than that?

He still had a few of yesterday's aches, and his head was sore from the knock he'd taken. Dressed only in pants, he padded into the kitchen and checked the water reservoir on the side of the elaborate cast-iron stove. The water in the zinc-lined tank was quite hot, and the tank was full.

He rummaged around in the big cabinets until he found the enamel bath. He got a bar of lye soap off the sink and pumped cold water to mix with the hot. His Colt lay on the chair next to him, on top of the towel.

The bath wasn't deep enough for him to stretch out in. Slocum vowed that one day he'd return to Brown's Hotel in Denver. They had a big, full-sized tub on every floor and a man who stayed inside the bathroom and kept it just as hot as you wanted, though you had to tip him two bits.

Sabrina said her good morning. John Slocum wasn't the first naked male she'd ever seen and wouldn't be the last. She was kind enough to scrub his back, although she felt obliged to make remarks about his general state of cleanliness and moral worth.

"John, it is so good to be inside again. I can feel the pressure of that winter, just like a live thing."

"What are those two doing out there?"

"They are bringing the sheep into pens. I think they hope to look them over and separate those that need more feeding or are hurt from the drive."

"They don't sound too happy," Slocum noted, because he could hear the voices quite clearly, and Mary Anne Murchison had just unloosed a string of curses a skinner might enjoy.

"They do not know how to herd the sheep and are

running them all over the pasture, and the sheep are so wild that they have broken through the fence in several places. The faster they ride their horses, the more frightened the sheep become, and several are dead from their exertions.''

"Not our job," Slocum said.

"I will help them," Sabrina said, "because I am hurt when I see animals mishandled.''

"I don't expect they'll ask in a real hurry," Slocum said. "Give that damn soap to me.''

" 'Please' give me the damn soap.''

"Please.''

Slocum had one set of clean clothes, his black gambler's outfit. He put his trail clothes into the same tub he'd previously occupied, with additional hot water and soap.

Beside the fire, he and Sabrina talked. Sabrina said Arnaud would not have wanted to be buried at Muleshoe. She corrected herself: "I do not wish him buried here because I do not wish to see Miss Murchison or her foreman whenever I come to visit his grave.''

"I think there's a church at Soda Springs. We can bury him there.''

"You said we would stay here a week.''

"It's very cold, Sabrina. The bodies will be . . . unchanged.''

Renfrew and Mary Anne stormed into the house; they were sweaty, and their blood was up. Mary Anne poured hot water into her teapot with trembling hands. Renfrew gawked at the black-clad man. "Jesus Christ,'' he said. "Will you look at him?''

John Slocum said, "I kept thinkin' I'm gonna have to teach you some manners."

"Ah hell!" Renfrew waved it away. "That black outfit. You surprised me, that's all. You look dressed for the last rites."

"Maybe I am."

"Yeah. Well, we're havin' a hell of a time out there, and we surely would appreciate your help."

Sabrina shrugged. "It will help pass the time," she said. "But you cannot have the use of Mr. Slocum unless you have some dry clothes to lend him. He must have this dark suit for Arnaud's funeral."

The remark was supposed to be funny, and Renfrew even gave it a smile. But Sabrina lost confidence and moisture came to her eyes, and she said, "Excuse me," and hurried out.

"We're close in size," Renfrew said. "I reckon I got something to fit."

Slocum picked a good tough pair of corduroys, a light cotton flannel shirt, and a rubberized slicker. The snow was still coming. It was sticking—building the first of the thick snow cover that'd gradually immobilize the ranch until spring.

Somebody was bound to die. Slocum could smell it in the air just as surely as he smelled the weather.

The little herding dogs shot out to Sabrina's command and soon had the scattered sheep gathered in the middle of the pasture.

The riders pressed against the sheep, with the dogs doing most of the work, until the lead sheep fed quietly into the sorting pens.

Forty at a time, they put them into the pens. The dogs sorted out the injured ones and held them aside while the healthy animals were hurried through. Renfrew was in the pasture scattering hay. The dogs wedged sheep together: hurt sheep, broken-legged sheep, sheep that were down at the mouth. Slocum reached over to take them by the neck and upend them for Sabrina's inspection. It was hard work— harder because Slocum wore pistols.

When a sheep sits upright, it can't struggle or fuss; it's paralyzed. While Slocum held, Sabrina made her decisions. She sorted the animals into those who needed to be fed, those who needed wounds cauterized, and those it wasn't worth saving. The last group was small, animals whose wounds were too severe or had the certain shocked look of animals gone terminal.

Mary Anne Murchison kept coming into the pen and going back out again until Slocum said, "Mary Anne, if you want to do this task, then you can do it. Me or Sabrina can scout for Jackson's bunch."

"You two are the only ones who know how to do it."

"They're your critters, Mary Anne, and you'd better learn something about them. You get that fool Renfrew in here and he can hold the woolies for a while. He must have that feed out by now."

While Renfrew took his place, John Slocum handed him the slicker. "You'll need this," he explained. "Wrestle with one or two and they'll wet you to the skin."

Renfrew was game to learn, but he was awful damn clumsy diving at the animals and wrestling them singly to the ground.

Patiently, Sabrina instructed him. Patiently, she

explained that Renfrew was doing harm to the sheep by handling them rough. Slocum watched for a while and it got no better. Renfrew was one of those men who are most stubborn when they are most ignorant.

After a sheep died from Renfrew's rough handling, Sabrina had had enough. "Señor," she said. "In my country when a male horse, a stallion, is too rough, too stupid, or too dangerous, we have a remedy." Her hand rested on the butt of her knife, and the look she gave him was all business.

He laughed because she was just a woman and nobody to tell him how to handle sheep or anything else for that matter.

Sabrina drew the long glittering blade and walked toward him on the balls of her feet.

His laugh broke. "Hey! I didn't mean—"

"Señor. You will be more gentle with these animals or you will become a gelding, and then you will be just as gentle as a lamb."

Slocum figured Sabrina was bluffing, but she put on a mighty good show. And Renfrew, sure as hell, didn't figure it was a bluff.

Slocum said, "I'm going to scout around a bit."

The snow would fill his tracks in thirty minutes. Visibility wasn't too good. Once he got a hundred yards from the pens, it was more like a wilderness than a settled place where men lived and did their work. Steadily, implacably, it snowed.

Slocum kept his Sharps .50 across his saddlebow and left his saddle holsters uncovered too, though that meant he'd need to pull the charges once he returned.

The ground was varied with sagebrush, tumbleweeds immobilized by the snow, and the hummocks and rises of the river-bottom hayfields. John Slocum rode out quite a way, almost a mile before he began his circle. He'd ride all around Muleshoe once.

Though his visibility closed down to fifty yards, within that charmed circle it was full of winter life. In some broken cattails beside the creek a wren had built her nest. Abandoned now, it hung by a thread of brown grass and old bird spit. The snow covered a small boulder and changed it into a buried cannonball. A few tracks upstream showed where ducks had landed and taken off again. These ducks were probably in a hell of a hurry to get south. Slocum rode his great circle, searching for the hoofprints of Teton Jackson's gang. John Slocum rode easy. But like some wild animal, he was alert to Jackson's presence, and if he didn't spot their tracks, by God, he'd smell them.

Three men. One wounded. Jackson, Wolfcoat, and Skinny. Those were the names Slocum had given them. They'd show no mercy when they came to take their revenge.

He shifted slightly in his saddle. Thought he saw something over there—but it was just a juniper draped with snow. It looked dark enough to be a man.

Slocum came on his own hoofprints before they were quite filled, and it pleased him he'd come out where he'd intended.

No sign of the enemy. . . .

Every day that passed without trouble made it more likely there wouldn't be any. Men couldn't live out in that storm very long without warmth and shelter.

The work went on at the pens. Bring forty fresh sheep into the pen, shed off the injured into a separate group. Press this group, and inspect the animals one by one. It was slow work.

They worked until it was too dark to examine the sheep properly, taking turns handling the animals for Sabrina's expert eye.

Mary Anne complained that they weren't even halfway done.

"This work, it does not happen overnight," Sabrina returned. She was tired too, and a little snippy.

"Next you'll be saying we need a Basque herder to handle the sheep," Mary Anne jeered.

Sabrina colored but held her retort. Dinner that night was canned pork heated in a skillet and quick-frying pan potatoes. Slocum opened a can of green beans and ate his portion cold. Hot or cold was all the same to him.

It was an awkward meal since nobody wanted to talk. Sabrina sat beside Slocum. Mary Anne and her foreman made a pair on the far side of the table. Renfrew grunted when he ate. Sabrina ate enough for two men—an appetite that surprised Slocum because she was such a slender woman.

They stacked and scraped their own dishes. Nobody wanted to do the work for the others.

In the living room Sabrina sat on one side of the big fireplace and the Muleshoe duo huddled in the far corner, making plans.

"Mr. Slocum." The note of triumph in Mary Anne's voice was unmistakable.

"Yeah."

"Jack and I will be sharing the same bedroom tonight."

Slocum was puzzled. The announcement wasn't peculiar, but the triumph was. "So?"

She smirked because she was giving her charms to another man. Renfrew held her hand smugly, like it was the handle of his possession.

"You have a real good time," Slocum said.

They hurried out of the room, whispering to each other.

Sabrina raised one eyebrow. "Are we so ridiculous?"

"Sometimes it seems so."

"And us?"

Slocum waited a while before he said, "I wasn't aware that we are an 'us.' "

She looked at him, bright eyes curious.

He wished he wasn't so taken by her. He wished he wasn't so taken by this strong hard-featured woman with the black hair.

Hell, what could he do—turn himself into a damn sheepherder like Arnaud? Would she help him manage his saloon or wander the backcountry with him?

"It'd never work," he said.

"Of course, John. We hardly know each other."

"I'm gonna turn down the lamps," he said. He went around the house locking the doors and checking the windows. One at a time he doused the kerosene lamps.

She hadn't gone anywhere and was waiting for him beside the great fireplace. She lay on a pile of overcoats on the floor in front of the fire. And her naked body was all shadows and sleekness.

"Come beside me, John," she said. "Whatever else we lack, we can have tonight."

They had that night and they had the next night and the night after that, on those mounds of clothing heaped before the glowing fireplace.

During the days they sorted sheep, and by the afternoon of the next day they were treating the hurt ones. Renfrew shot the hopeless cases, and he and Slocum skinned out the pelts. If the meat was young enough and not awful gaunt, they kept the loin and the hams. Soon they had a dozen mutton hams hanging high from the front porch where they'd be good until it got warm again.

Sabrina never went near the wagon that held her brother. She acted as if he had been buried for years.

In the drowsiness after sex, in the rusty glow of the firelight, she and John Slocum exchanged secrets. They got to know each other, and every surprise they found in each other was more marvelous than the last.

Renfrew and Mary Anne. Sabrina and Slocum. They were like two factions at a political convention, working together for the good of the party. They hated each other's guts.

As the work went on, Slocum made shorter rounds around the ranchouse. The snow was two feet deep, and the wind was blowing the crust into edges that would cut a horse's leg to the bone. Every hour lessened the chances of Jackson being alive. He must have gone on to Soda Springs. That's what everybody was thinking, though nobody actually said that aloud, because saying would bring bad luck.

Of course Teton Jackson was very much alive and very bad luck indeed.

That night the sky was clear for a change. Plenty of stars blinked, and the moon was three days from full and huge above the floodlit valley and the barns and the house. Three riders rode through the flock of sheep. The sheep had bedded where they'd been fed and were completely incurious about the three men who rode, one and then two side by side.

One man was whispering—the skinny one. He whispered, "Fuck you Muleshoe. Oh, fuck you. Oh, your murderous, murderous, murderous people . . ."

The whisper as the horses crunched steadily through the snow. One of the horses stumbled, because except for twigs and dead bushes, they'd had nothing to eat since Wyoming.

Teton Jackson's horse was dying between his legs, and he didn't give a damn.

Wolfcoat led his horse as often as he rode it, and he didn't give a damn either.

They took the main road directly through the hayfield and past the horse barns and they didn't speak, just the ferocious whispering and the crunch of their horses.

The guard dogs were dead. The little herding dogs hurried out from their den under the buckboard. When Teton Jackson climbed down from his horse, they ran back underneath, whimpering. Jackson had something shiny in his hands, enormous muzzle. Triggers wired down. His sawed-off Greener.

He stood before the ranchhouse. Since Skinny's whispering had become their marching music for the past three days and nights, Teton Jackson didn't think to ask for silence now.

They smelled the chimney smoke from the house. Saw the ripples in the night above its stone mouth. They could smell tobacco smoke and they could smell mutton steaks. Teton Jackson drooled.

Like automatons, they marched around the corner of the ranchhouse. Teton Jackson paused at each window and every door. His men waited respectfully behind him.

He'd just reached the window of Mary Anne's room, where Renfrew and Mary Anne were sleeping, when the herding dogs regained their courage and started to bark as if their lives depended on raising the alarm.

Teton Jackson shoved glass window inside the house, where it fell, frame and all, across Mary Anne's bed. Like a stinking gorilla, he crawled in through the space he'd made, onto the rag rug Mary Anne Murchison had sewn herself when she was just sixteen.

Renfrew sat up in bed so fast that the window frame crashed off the end of the bed.

Mary Anne Murchison screamed. Wolfcoat was filling the window now. He grunted with the effort.

Mary Anne babbled, "You can have them. You can have the sheep. You can have Muleshoe. Anything you want . . ."

Teton Jackson turned his ghastly face to hers. "We'll only be wanting your lives," he said.

"Hey, I know this dude," Wolfcoat said as the moonlight fell across Renfrew's frightened face. "He was the one . . . that time old Red Smart, he . . . I don't remember. Where'd I see you, mister?''

He bent close. He stank of his own stink and the stink of his body eating itself. Teton Jackson had boiled their saddlebags for soup last night.

. All three were starved and gaunt. Jackson's nose was frostibitten from tip to the splay of his nostrils, dead white and already sluffing skin in ugly white strips. Wolfcoat's left hand was rotten. He'd lost his glove and couldn't keep it warm. For three nights they'd cowered in snow caves they'd dug during the waning of the evening.

Skinny whispered his whisper as he came into Mary Anne Murchison's bedroom. His right side was stiff—something wrong with his arm too. He kicked over a row of Mary Anne's childhood toys.

She was frightened speechless.

''I . . . I was Murchison's foreman.'' Renfrew wanted to help the man leaning over him, wanted to help very much. ''Up in the mountains. I surrendered to you.''

Wolfcoat said, ''Surrendered? Hell, what are you gonna do? You're in that bed all covered with glass, and, by God, you're both buck naked. Buck naked. Oh, we'll have some use for this one. Teton, look at the goddamned tits on her.''

Mary Anne said, ''Jack . . . Jack, please!''

Jack Renfrew didn't move a muscle.

Teton Jackson had his face to a crack in the door. ''John Slocum,'' he called. ''I got your boss-lady in here and another one of your bunch. I'm gonna start whittlin' on 'em. I thought you'd like to know that.''

He turned back to Wolfcoat. "If those damn dogs hadn't started to yelp, we'd have them dead."

"I'll shoot 'em," Skinny said. "I'll shoot the dogs. It's bright as day out there. If I shoot 'em they won't make no more noise." When Skinny stuck his arm outside, his pistol was shaking so bad he couldn't get aim.

"Naw," Jackson said. "Let the damn dogs live. We'll kill these two. We'll kill Slocum and we'll kill that other girl. That's all we have to do. We don't have to go on and kill a couple yappy dogs." He turned his muzzle toward the bed and dropped the hammers. The blast hurt everybody's eyes, but Jack Renfrew's worst of all. The shock of the blast pushed the bed back against the wall, and those balls that didn't hit Jack bit into the mattress. The room filled with powder smoke, blood flecks, and goosedown feathers.

"Jesus," Skinny said. "Jesus," he said again. "You killed the damn girl, too."

Jackson leaned near. "Naw," he said. "She's just fainted. He bent to the doorway again. "Slocum, that was one of your pals. You want us to kill the other one?"

Long silence. Down the hallway he heard nothing. It'd be the living room down there. Even his befuddled brain could figure that out. It was too damn warm in this place. He felt the pull of his weariness. He'd come so far following his tormentors. So very far.

Wolfcoat said, "Let's kill 'em. Me, I'll go around to the front and we'll have them caught between . . . We'll . . ." He shrugged. He knew what he meant to say but couldn't find words for it. One exhausted outlaw crawled out of the window and began his slow march around the side of the house. Teton would wait for a while and then come out shooting.

Wolfcoat actually saw the woman. Saw she was beautiful. He thought he had her identified, thought he knew her, and then her thrown knife took him right in the breast and the point cut through the bone, and when he gasped, half the air went out of him from his collapsed lung and he toppled into the snow.

Teton Jackson and Skinny ran down the narrow hall. It was a very stupid thing to do.

Side by side they rushed down that long hall and burst into the living room firing and one of Jackson's bullets ruined J.D. Murchison's chair and another embedded itself in the bookcase. Skinny broke the front window.

Slocum fired exactly twice and two men set forth on the slow, serious work of dying. John Slocum waited in the kitchen doorway with his pistol in his hand and the smoke curling out of the barrel, and Teton Jackson died just where Slocum and Sabrina had made love.

Her hand was ice cold when she put it on his wrist. "It is very cold outside," she said. "But it does not smell so bad as in here."

She led the way.

Wolfcoat lay where Sabrina's knife had left him. He looked like any other dead furry landscape.

"We are accursed," she said.

John Slocum looked out at the country, washed in the brightness of the moon. He could feel the moonlight devouring his soul.

**GREAT WESTERN YARNS FROM ONE OF THE
BEST-SELLING WRITERS IN THE FIELD TODAY**

582-22

JAKE LOGAN